FRANKLIN DELANO ROOSEVELT

Champion of Freedom

Illustrated by Meryl Henderson

FRANKLIN DELANO ROOSEVELT

Champion of Freedom

by Kathleen Kudlinski

ALADDIN PAPERBACKS

New York London Toronto Sydney Singapore

For my mother-in-law,
Ann Kudlinski,
with thanks for sharing
stories of life in the
Depression and
her work as a real
Rosie the Riveter
in a defense plant.

Note: A portion of the proceeds
from this book is being donated
by the author to the fight against
polio.

First Aladdin Paperbacks edition September 2003
Text copyright © 2003 by Kathleen Kudlinski
Illustrations copyright © 2003 by Meryl Henderson

Aladdin Paperbacks
An imprint of Simon & Schuster Children's Publishing Division
1230 Avenue of the Americas
New York, NY 10020

Designed by Lisa Vega
The text of this book was set in Adobe Garamond.

Manufactured in the United States of America
6 8 10 9 7 ˉ

Library of Congress Control Number 2002107420
ISBN-13: 978-0-689-85745-4
ISBN-10: 0-689-85745-4
0513 OFF

ILLUSTRATIONS

CONTENTS

"Without Fuss"

"Good morning, Master Roosevelt." The gardener tipped his hat to Franklin. "You surely do ride well for a seven-year-old."

Franklin just grinned and kicked his pony to a faster trot. His big black dog, Monk, barked with joy and romped alongside. Together they paraded across the front lawn of Springwood, the Roosevelt estate in Hyde Park, New York. Franklin was glad to be out for the hour of play after a long morning at lessons with his tutor. At the edge of their lawn, the broad Hudson River glinted in the afternoon sun. Franklin slid off Debbie's back and left the pony grazing on the new spring grasses while he walked down to the water.

He checked the knots holding their boats to the dock. A steamboat paddled up the river, belching smoke. Skiffs and sloops, a ketch and a schooner hauled at their sails, steering wide to give the big boat extra space. Franklin leaned over to drag his fingers through the water and grinned. The Hudson was still too cold for swimming, but the breeze was perfect for sailing. His father would be home for tea soon, he thought. Franklin jumped to his feet, wondering what his "Popsy" had planned for them for the afternoon.

He glanced up the long sloping riverbank to the huge old farmhouse at the top of the ridge. The sun reflected in its windows, hiding the bustle of maids and cooks, the nanny and the tutor inside. He squinted. His mother was standing, silent and still, on the front porch. He loved how she looked in her fine dresses.

Franklin waved and she gestured calmly for him to come in. When he ran up onto the porch, she said simply, "I have news." He followed his mother into her study, being careful not to step on the edges of her long skirt. Monk followed too, quiet now.

Mother sat down at her desk and folded her hands in her lap. Franklin sat on a satin chair nearby. "What is it, Mother?" he asked, when he couldn't stand to wait any longer.

"Archibald Rogers has died, dear."

"Archibald is dead? When?" Franklin pictured his best friend and blinked hard to hold back tears. "But, Mother, we play together every week! What happened to Archibald? Tell me!"

"Now, Franklin." Franklin froze at the tone in her voice. Mother didn't like it when he made a fuss. He took a shuddering breath and stared up at the portrait of his ancestor, Isaac Roosevelt. The painting had hung in Franklin's home as long as he could remember. ISAAC

ROOSEVELT, 1726–1794. Franklin recited the portrait's label to himself from memory. NEW YORK'S FIRST STATE SENATOR. It helped him to quiet down. So did Isaac's stern, proud gaze.

"Archibald died of diphtheria, Son." Franklin winced at his mother's words. That was one of the awful illnesses that his parents worried about—scarlet fever, polio, measles, appendicitis, pneumonia, diptheria. There were many more. "This is most unfortunate indeed," Mrs. Roosevelt said. Franklin slid from his chair and went to stand by her. "One would think," she said, "that by 1889 they would have found a cure." Franklin wiped his eyes and his mother went on. "Young Archibald was one of the few suitable playmates for you in Hyde Park."

"With whom will I play, Mother?"

"Archibald had a brother, didn't he? He would be suitable. And our guests at dinner parties are always glad to speak with you,

Franklin. And there are always the relatives."

Franklin wanted a hug. He threw his arms around Monk and squeezed, then leaned his cheek against the dog's shaggy fur to feel the animal's warmth. Monk's tail thumped against the elegant silk carpet. Mrs. Roosevelt looked sharply at the big dog, but said nothing. Franklin loosened his arms around the dog. It licked him as he stood up. Franklin cleared his throat and stared at the Bible on the shelf below the portrait. His name was in there. The big old book was written in Dutch. It had been passed down through the family for generations and every birth and death and marriage was recorded there. He concentrated, trying to picture his page and its spidery writing: *Franklin Delano Roosevelt, born January 30, 1882.* All of his famous family was in there. And all of the others who had died, Franklin thought. Of diseases. Of diphtheria. He swallowed hard.

"Come here, dear," Mrs. Roosevelt said.

"You may help me with my stamp collection." Franklin leaned over her shoulder and looked at the stamps spread across her desk. They seemed to melt together in the tears that filled his eyes. He sniffed, but quietly.

"Look at this one, Franklin," Mrs. Roosevelt said. "It is from Great Britain, and that is a picture of the English queen, Victoria. She has ruled that country and dozens of others in her commonwealth for fifty-two years now." Franklin stared at the woman on the stamp. It was interesting to think that someone had held power for so long.

"Would you like to hold the stamp?" Franklin could not believe it when Mother handed him the tweezers. She turned on the new electric light and let him look through her hand lens at the woman who ruled countries. Then Mrs. Roosevelt gave him a little folded mounting patch and let him lick one side and glue it to the back of the stamp. Franklin looked at her. She nodded and then pointed to the spot where the stamp fit into her huge album.

Franklin wanted to shout for joy. He had never been allowed to touch her stamps before! He tried to keep his hand from trembling as he licked the other side of the patch and tried to center the stamp in the square Mother had shown him. Franklin held his breath and felt the glue stick to the paper. It was perfect!

Mother gave his shoulder a warm pat.

"Pardon me." They looked up. Franklin's new governess stood in the doorway, her ruffled apron starkly white against her long navy dress. "Master Roosevelt? The tutor is ready for your German lesson."

Not now! Franklin almost groaned aloud, but caught himself in time.

"Franklin dear," Mother said, "you may spend time with your Popsy this afternoon at four o'clock. He is expecting to sail with you. Now kiss me and go on." She tilted her head to offer her cheek. With a last glance at the stamp album, Franklin kissed his mother and followed his governess out.

"Ahoy there!" Franklin called to his parents, three years later and hundreds of miles north of Hyde Park. He trimmed the sails on his family's boat and eased it alongside the dock at their summer home.

"Right-o!" Popsy called from the shore.

Mother clapped. Franklin tied off the line and stared for a moment at his parents. Mother looked so elegant in her straw hat. Popsy looked far older than any of his friends' fathers. His silver hair shone in the Canadian sun. How Franklin had missed them! He leaped to the dock and raced up the path.

"What else did you see in Germany?" his mother asked as they sat sunning in the lawn chairs.

"Soldiers, Mother. Lots of soldiers."

"What else would a ten-year-old see?"

Mother asked. "I would prefer to hear of art works you saw, government offices you visited, or people whom you met."

Popsy laughed loudly. "Sara, that can wait. I should think our young man would rather run off the length of the island while the day is fair." He winked at Franklin. "Later we can discuss—perhaps in German—your son's six weeks abroad."

Franklin looked from one parent to the other, then grinned. "I'll be back for supper." He headed off to roam the piney woods and marshes of Campobello Island. Across the bay, he could see Maine and the boat that ferried them over from the mainland every spring. The other side of the island faced the open Atlantic. Between, there were miles of paths and hollows, ponds and boulder castles to explore. Tides surged in and out all around the island, their currents swifter than the Hudson River at flood stage. He had wasted so many weeks away, and so many weeks sailing on the ocean liner back and forth from New York City to Germany! He ran faster, to catch up on his summer.

Suddenly a stick cracked under his foot. One end of it whipped up and slammed him in the face. Franklin grabbed his mouth with both his hands. *Pain!* It screamed through his jaw. Pain filled his mind, his thoughts. He staggered backward trying to make sense of the blood and rocks in his mouth. He spit out a whole tooth, but the pain was worse where he'd almost broken off another.

Franklin spit and swallowed until the bleeding had nearly stopped. He splashed cold pond water on his face. The cuts stung, the place for his missing tooth ached, but the live nerve in the broken tooth screamed every time air touched it. He trudged home, trying to think what he would say to his parents. They had plans. Campobello Island and the cabins were for fun, not for dentist's visits.

But that was where he had to go. Mrs.

Roosevelt took Franklin to the ferry dock, his face swelling, his head aching, and his mouth in pain beyond anything he had ever felt. Franklin did not let himself cry. He wouldn't even complain. He blinked back tears and tried to keep his swollen lips shut on the ferry passage. He stayed silent at the dentist's and through the trip back to the island.

By the time he returned to the supper table, he was dizzy with pain and painkillers. The piney smell of the cabin's warm wooden walls and the cozy light of candles and lanterns helped him to relax. Fire crackled in the fireplace. There were no satin chairs here, no tasseled drapes or antique portraits, but this was home, as much as Hyde Park. Franklin felt the comfort all through his body.

"Here you are, Master Roosevelt." The cook set a plate of mashed potatoes before him. The Roosevelts had brought her to Campobello from Springwood, along with tutors and maids. Franklin looked up at her kind face and smiled. Campobello was the one place where manners were relaxed. They could have picnic food here, right at the table. His favorite was hot dogs. Even the thought now of chewing one hurt his mouth, so he quietly said his thank-you for the plate of soft, mushy potatoes.

"You would have been proud of your son," Mrs. Roosevelt said to her husband. "Please," she paused while the cook served her plate. "Franklin is such a stubborn little Dutchman that he went through the whole thing without a fuss." There was love in her voice, and it made Franklin's mouth feel better just to hear it.

"What would you expect?" Popsy said. "He's a Roosevelt!"

Franklin sat taller and ate as much of the potatoes as he could.

"Ready to ride?" Popsy said at Hyde Park, one afternoon the next winter.

Franklin laughed aloud. "Always!" he crowed. They hurried to the stables behind the house and looked in on the Roosevelt horses. Walking down the long hall, they stopped at each stall as Popsy described the trotter's racing victories. After the Roosevelts picked their afternoon's mounts, the groom hurried to saddle the horses.

The dull gray sky threatened snow, and clouds of steam formed from the horses' breaths—Monk's and the Roosevelts', too. "Snow is good for the crops," Popsy explained as they trotted past empty fields and orchards. "It keeps the hard cold from the roots."

They tied the horses to the fence and slogged through the old snow to check the places where they had grafted trees. Back in the spring, they had slit the barks on a few trees, then slid twigs from a new kind of pear into the mature trees. The wrappings of wax and burlap were still in place. Franklin grinned. The grafts would grow. Within the next few years there would be two different kinds of pears hanging on each tree!

"They'll get a good watering when the snow melts," Mr. Roosevelt said. "They'll need it."

"I know all that, Popsy," Franklin laughed. "Every day you tell me about nature and farming. Every day I listen."

"Would you want me to stop?" Mr. Roosevelt asked.

Franklin grinned. "I don't think you could!"

Popsy laughed. "You are right. The land, the plants, the river—all of it is in my blood."

"And mine," Franklin said. They rode on in silence until a grouse flew up suddenly from the dead grasses by the road.

"That reminds me, Son," Mr. Roosevelt said. "Your eleventh birthday is next week, and I have my eye on a fine shotgun for you." Franklin stared at his father and held his breath in anticipation. "Yes," the old man said, "but there are some rules you must agree to."

"Anything." Franklin breathed. His own

gun! He could hunt like his cousin Theodore.

"Take no more than one bird of each species," Popsy said, "and not during nesting seasons. And you must keep records."

"I already do that for my nest collection, Popsy, and the birds' eggs I have blown out and dried. I have notebooks and charts and—"

"If you weren't already a naturalist," Popsy interrupted, "I would not have offered this."

Franklin shivered as the first wet snowflakes blew across the meadow. His teeth were chattering. "I think we should stop by the greenhouse, Popsy. Wouldn't Mother like a fresh flower?"

Mr. Roosevelt laughed. "You just want an excuse to get warm!"

Franklin kicked his mount into a canter and they raced to the greenhouse.

In the end, Mrs. Roosevelt got her flower.

"Mother!" Franklin burst through the front door of the Hyde Park home three years later, followed by his tutor. Monk bounded into the hall and slid to a stop against Franklin's knees. "I'm home!" Franklin lowered his voice quickly as his mother came from her room and presented her cheek for a welcoming kiss. "Popsy sent his own railroad car for me in New York!" he said. "What a relief. I'm tuckered out from the trip. Do you know what it is like to pedal a bicycle all over Europe?"

"It is precisely what a fourteen-year-old needs, Franklin. Exercise . . . and exposure."

"Oh, but it was wonderful, Mother!" Franklin couldn't stop bubbling.

"Save your stories," Mrs. Roosevelt said. "Your cousins are all coming for supper tonight—almost twenty of them. And your father is waiting for you on the tennis courts." Franklin looked all around the grand front hall. It was different somehow.

"Oh, Mother!" he gasped. The birds he had shot had been stuffed and mounted in a glass case in the wall. He stepped over to look at them. The woodpeckers were there, the cardinal, the oriole, the ducks, and even the tiny chickadee. They were posed to look life-like. "Oh, Mother," he said again. "Thank you."

"You are quite welcome," Mrs. Roosevelt said. "I also steamed the stamps off the notes your tutor sent from Europe for your collection. You will find them in your bedroom."

Franklin took the stairs two at a time, then stopped in surprise at his doorway. His mother had redecorated his room again while he was gone. He grinned and shook his head. On his new desk lay his stamp albums and several formal-looking letters. Franklin looked closer. They were from Groton School. "Later," he told them, and changed into his white tennis slacks and sweater and grabbed a racket. Trying not to think about the fall—and the boarding school he would have to attend—Franklin ran back down the stairs, out the door, and down the lawn to the clay tennis courts.

He stopped, looking at his father. Popsy looked old to him, older than he remembered. "My boy!" Mr. Roosevelt cried, and swept him into a bear hug. "Ready to lose?"

"Never!" Franklin said.

"That's my boy," Mr. Roosevelt laughed. He patted him with a racket and jogged to the far side of the court.

Mrs. Roosevelt walked across the grass with a parasol to sit in the sun and watch.

"Your serve, Franklin," Popsy said.

School

The tall spire of St. John's Chapel was the first sight Franklin had of his new home at Groton School, an hour's ride from Boston, Massachusetts. As his parents hurried the carriage around the great, circular drive at the school, Franklin stared. There were boys everywhere. Some were kicking at balls on the sports field, some were carrying suitcases or trunks, and others were saying good-bye to their parents or waving hello to old school friends. No one waved at Franklin.

While his baggage waited in the carriage

with the coachman, the Roosevelts climbed the steps of an enormous redbrick building. A boy in the Groton School uniform held the door open for them, and Mrs. Roosevelt swept in. "Thank you," Franklin said, but the boy just stared at him.

"Wait here, please," a secretary said. Franklin perched on an elegant leather chair and watched Mother and Popsy disappear into the headmaster's office. The secretary sat down at her desk and busied herself writing. Franklin stared at the walls. The school's crest was everywhere. It showed three open books over a sword on a white cross. CUI SERVIRE EST REGNARE—the school's motto was written across the bottom. "In whose service is perfect freedom." Franklin translated the Latin easily. He knew languages. He had traveled to Europe eight times. His mother had taught him to read by the age of four. Since then he'd had the very best tutors. Why, he wondered, did he have to go to school at all?

He knew the answer. Mother had explained it over and over. It was 1896 and going to the right school was important for his future. Then he had to go to the right college. He had to meet the right people, too, Mother had said. The sounds of laughter floated in from the hallway. Franklin moved to stand in the doorway.

"You don't suppose *he*"—a boy in a Groton sweater glanced at Franklin then looked back at his friends—"expects to be a student *here*?" All three of the students laughed.

"He'd better not be on the fourth form football team," one of them said. "He's too light. Too small."

Franklin tried to stand taller.

"Peabody will set him right," a third boy said, and they all chuckled nervously. Franklin swallowed. Peabody was the headmaster. What sort of man was going to be in charge of him, once his parents left? The boys glanced around the hall.

Franklin knew his manners, even if these Groton students didn't. He would not show fear—or anger, either. "My name is Franklin Delano Roosevelt," he said, extending his hand. "And you would be . . . ?"

"Oh, my!" one of the boys said. "Where is this little Franklin from? His accent sounds German. Or British. Where did you go to school, little one?"

Franklin felt his face flush. None of the friends he'd had at Hyde Park had ever been this rude. He pulled his hand back and one of the boys laughed again.

"Oh, leave off." The tallest boy scolded the others into silence.

Franklin had just nodded his thanks to the tall boy when the secretary called out, "Master Roosevelt? The headmaster will see you now."

"Reverend Endicott Peabody." The big man's handshake was warm and solid. So was his smile. "Welcome to Groton, Master Roosevelt." Franklin felt his shoulders relax.

24

"We expect you to do well here and go on to become a leader in America."

Franklin looked at his parents. Had they told him to say that? "Our students come from wealthy, privileged families like yours, Franklin. We expect them all to enter public service," Reverend Peabody said. He glanced down at a paper. "You've come to us with an excellent academic background. We have decided to slip you into third-year studies here. In public school it would be called 'tenth grade.' Here it is called 'fourth form.' Academics at Groton are important, but so are social and moral growth."

"My Franklin," Mrs. Roosevelt interrupted, "will have no social problems. He has always been quick to make friends with suitable young men."

"I'm sure, Mrs. Roosevelt," the headmaster said, "but nearly all of the students your son's age entered Groton two years ago. They all know each other well and may challenge a new boy before offering friendship."

Franklin grinned to himself. "I see your son may have encountered this already," the headmaster said. Franklin stared at him, amazed. He'd always been told that children were to be seen and not heard. But adults didn't usually bother to see them any more than listen to them.

"You must come in and speak with me whenever the door is open, Franklin, if you should have any problems or questions. The boys all know they are welcome at any time." The man's intense blue eyes were so kind and sincere that Franklin knew he already had one friend at Groton. "Every morning the students assemble in the chapel," Reverend Endicott told the Roosevelts.

"Is everyone here of the Episcopalian faith?" Mr. Roosevelt asked.

"No. And though I offer a weekly confirmation class for those who want it, many students never participate."

"May I sign up, please, sir?" Franklin tried

to imagine a class every week with this nice man. His parents looked stunned, but the headmaster smiled.

"Of course. You should know that there is a good deal of service to the community involved beyond that already required of our students." Franklin nodded. Work away from the school—and the Groton boys—sounded good to Franklin.

"Well, then," Reverend Peabody said, "all this leaves is athletics. What sport will you choose for afternoon exercise?"

"Tennis," Franklin said.

"I am sorry. Groton boys do not play tennis."

"Sailing, then? Or riding? Golf?" Franklin thought of the sports he knew well.

"We play only team sports here at Groton. They build teamwork and cooperation as well as coordination," the headmaster said. He looked down at his books and wrote something. "Since you have no preference, I am signing you up for football."

❖ ❖ ❖ ❖

It took Franklin years to fit in at Groton. He listened carefully to the accent most of the other students had. He practiced dropping his *r*'s and making his *a* sound broad and flat. When he said, "a train car in the yard," it sounded more like, "a train cah in the yahd." Finally he could talk just like they did. His mother and father had always expected him to hide his deepest feelings—he had gotten very good at that. Now he polished a shell of humor and boldness to cover everything that was going on inside.

When the other boys teased him about being too good, Franklin made just enough noise in class to get a black mark on his record. He never made the school baseball team, so he became the team's manager instead. The hours he spent in classes and study seemed boring, though his grades were acceptable. And though he entered Groton School small and thin, he grew seven inches in four years. The afternoon exercise period gave him muscle bulk and strength and grace.

Franklin won a prize in Latin and was one of the school's star debaters, but those honors meant little compared to Franklin's service projects. As part of Groton's missionary society, he was sent to care for a poor black woman. Week after week throughout one winter, Franklin brought baskets of food to her in the poorest section of Boston. Time and again, he brought fuel so the woman would not freeze. He brought clothes and friendship, too.

He got much more in return. He had to see—and care—about people who lived without maids or summer homes or private train cars. He saw that thousands of people didn't have even enough coal to warm their fingers, let alone their rooms. With every trip Franklin was forced to see real hunger. Now when he looked at his classmates, Franklin knew how lucky they all were. He knew how lucky *he* was.

One summer Franklin volunteered at a camp for underprivileged boys. The little boys loved the tall, handsome Franklin. He played rough-and-tumble games with them and listened to their stories. He also worked at a club for poor children in downtown Boston.

"Will you join me in my rounds?" the teacher in charge of the Missionary Society invited Franklin. With Reverend Sherrard Billings, Franklin visited hospitals and people's homes all over the area near Groton. These were not poor people, but they certainly were not "people of wealth and privilege," either. They were somewhere in the middle, a middle class that Franklin had never known before. Together Franklin and the reverend listened to people's worries and hopes, arranged help, and gave comfort wherever they could.

Headmaster Peabody tried everything to get his students interested in public service. He invited politicians and speakers to give talks in the chapel. One evening Franklin's cousin Theodore Roosevelt came to speak to the Groton students.

Theodore told wonderful stories about the fire department and the police that he knew from being on the police board. These were not the quiet stories of missionaries, but tales of danger and gore, excitement and heroism. Franklin wanted his cousin's kind of public service. He was thrilled when Theodore invited him to spend the Fourth of July with his branch of the family out at Oyster Bay, New York.

By the time Franklin was nearing graduation from Groton, he had made up his mind. "I am going into the navy!" he wrote to his parents. "A friend and I are going to run away to Boston to enlist. Don't try to stop me. The Spanish-American War has begun, and my country needs me."

The Roosevelts did not stop Franklin.

Scarlet fever did. He was far too sick to sneak into Boston and too sick to be of any use to the navy.

Next Franklin decided to apply to the navy's military college, Annapolis. When he graduated he could enter the service as an officer. Then he could sail all the world's oceans just as he had sailed the family's fifty-one-foot sailing boat on the Hudson River and the channels around Campobello Island. He imagined himself at the wheel of a military ship, winning sea battles. He told himself that his parents would be happy with this plan. Hadn't they often told him about his grandfather's adventures in the China trade? They had even urged him to spend time in the Delano's attic, reading old logbooks from whaling ships.

"No," said Mother, when he told her about his plan to be a leader on the high seas. Mrs. Roosevelt explained the plan that she and his father had for his future. "You will go to

Harvard," she announced. Franklin did not bother to fight. All Roosevelt men went to Harvard. He knew that. They all went on to brilliant careers and lives of great wealth and comfort in high society. He had known all his life what his parents wanted from him. There was no one else to fulfill their dreams. How could he let them down?

"And after Harvard," Mother plowed on, "you will become a lawyer. From there, you could enter politics. And," Mrs. Roosevelt said, as she always did, "I expect you to be very successful."

"Yes, Mother," Franklin agreed.

Inside he vowed to fulfill his own dreams, too.

Following the Plan

"Hi, Franklin!" It was easy for Franklin to feel at home at Harvard University when he arrived in 1900. Several of his friends from Groton sat together at tables in the private dining room saved for Groton graduates. "Sit with us!" they called to him. Older Groton students who had been going to Harvard for years were friendly, too. They could tell the new boys about the school and show them around Cambridge and Boston, Massachusetts. It helped to have the right contacts at college, just as Mrs. Roosevelt had said. During his last years of high school, Franklin had learned how to make friends, and now he used these new skills.

While attending Harvard, Franklin lived with Groton graduates in an off-campus apartment in an expensive neighborhood in Cambridge instead of living in the dormitories. Clubs, dances, and Harvard's social life took most of Franklin's attention. Because he had such good study skills, Franklin was able to earn passable grades and have good times, too. The classes he chose included courses in economics. His professors taught that the federal government's controls on business and banking could help keep the economy healthy. It was a new idea to him—one his parents and family would not agree with.

They would have been happy, however, to see him marching in a torchlight parade for Theodore Roosevelt. Franklin's cousin Teddy was running for vice president of the United States. William McKinley was running for president. When the Young Republican Club planned a political rally, Franklin was quick to join in, though he was a Democrat. It was thrilling to march with hundreds of other students, shouting and cheering the Roosevelt name. Their flaming torches lit the dark streets and flickered wildly on the upturned faces of the marchers. Had it been like this when his ancestor Isaac Roosevelt ran for office? Franklin wondered.

He listened whenever Theodore stopped and made speeches. He joined the crowds in the wild applause. Then they all marched on, their numbers growing as they followed cousin Theodore for eight miles through the streets. At the end of the night Franklin went back to the apartment filled with a passion for politics. William McKinley went on to win the election and his cousin Theodore moved to Washington.

Franklin led several clubs in college and was chosen to be the editor of the Harvard

newspaper. Franklin played for sports teams and became a manager, too, practicing his leadership skills. For the first time in his life he was popular with classmates—and with women, too. Handsome and rich, with a cousin who was the vice president, Franklin began to think he could have anything he wanted.

Popsy died while Franklin was away at college. Franklin's elderly father had been ill, so his death was not a surprise—but it was a sorrow. Mrs. Roosevelt shifted her life's focus to her only son. She spent the next two winters in Boston to be near Franklin while he studied.

Franklin dated many women during his first days in college. Over time he fell in love with one named Alice. Franklin remembered growing up as the only child in the house, longing for brothers or sisters to play with. He wanted to have a big, happy family. Alice said no to his plan of six children, and no to Franklin. He went on looking for a woman to share his dream.

✿ ✿ ✿ ✿

Every man at Harvard wanted to belong to
the Porcellian. This club was full of people
Franklin thought would be helpful to him
later as a politician. The only way to get into
the Porcellian was by a secret vote of the members. Franklin let the men know he wanted to
join. Then he waited for his invitation knowing
it was a sure thing. The invitation never came.

Franklin could not believe he had lost the
membership vote. Some of his friends must
have voted against him! He couldn't argue or
charm or buy his way into the club either.
Losing was a new feeling for Franklin, and he
hated it. As always, he kept his feelings quiet,
moving on without a fuss.

Theodore Roosevelt became president in
1901 when William McKinley was assassi-
nated. Now Franklin's cousin was living in the
White House. Franklin visited him several
times for family parties. At these parties he
began talking to Eleanor Roosevelt. Eleanor

was serious, pretty, and very smart. She was honest and open about her feelings in a way that fascinated the secretive Franklin. She, too, was a relative of Theodore's—his niece. The more they talked, the more Franklin realized how alike they were.

Eleanor was interested in public service. She worked with poor women and children, as Franklin had in high school. She had lived a lonely childhood. Both her mother and father had died before she was eleven, and she was raised by stern, elderly relatives. She, too, longed for a big, happy family.

Eleanor agreed to meet Franklin for dates in New York City where she lived. Instead of picking her up at her lovely apartment, she had him come to different housing shelters where she worked. Franklin had to see poverty and troubles—truths he had almost forgotten in the wealthy glitter of his Harvard life. He knew that a national politician had to stay in touch with what the poor and middle-class people were thinking. Eleanor could help. She believed in him and in his dreams, too. Franklin asked her to marry him in 1903 and Eleanor said yes.

Franklin was sure that his mother would be happy. He was wrong. "How could you, Franklin!" Mrs. Roosevelt scolded. "You have a future! How could you even think of getting married now—and to *her*?" She didn't even use Eleanor's name. "You need to concentrate on your studies. After graduate school you need to focus on making your mark in the world. Then, and only then," she said, "you might choose a wife. One"—her voice deepened—"who will *help* your career." She pressed her lips together.

Franklin handled his mother as he always did. He nodded and seemed to agree, and kept his own plan secret. He promised to wait until after graduating before marrying Eleanor.

"Thank you, dear," she said. "We have to

think about your destiny, you know." She patted her son's shoulder. "You'll see. You'll soon
lose interest in *her*." Franklin knew better,
but he did not bother to argue.

Near the end of his time at Harvard, he
decided to become a lawyer. He applied to
study at Columbia University Law School in
New York City. They were glad to welcome the
president's nephew. In 1904 Franklin voted
for the first time. Franklin was a Democrat,
but for this vote, he chose the Republican
candidate, Theodore. Franklin and Eleanor
were in Washington to see Teddy Roosevelt
sworn in as president for a second term.

The spring after Franklin graduated from
Harvard, he married Eleanor on Saint Patrick's
Day in 1905 in New York City. Their wedding
was a huge society event. Two cousins of the
president were marrying—and Teddy was
giving the bride away! Newspapers and
magazines covered the wedding and the
speeches that Theodore made afterward.

The newlyweds left on a long trip to Europe.

By the time they got back, Franklin's mother had their wedding gift ready: Mrs. Roosevelt had bought and furnished side-by-side townhouses in New York City. One was for her. The other was for the young couple. Mrs. Roosevelt had already moved into hers, and it had a sliding door that opened right into the newlyweds' home. She used that door often.

One day Franklin found Eleanor crying in the bedroom. "What on earth is the matter with you?" he asked.

"I wanted my own house," she sobbed.

"This is our house," he said, confused.

"But *I* wanted to pick out curtains for us, and wallpaper and furniture and carpets. I want my own china on the table!" She waved her hand around the room. "This is not mine. It isn't the way I wanted to live."

"I don't understand." Franklin looked at the heavy, tasseled drapes, the dark carpet, and the expensive bedspread. It was as beautiful as anything at Hyde Park. "Don't you like what Mother picked for us?" Eleanor just buried her face in her hands. Franklin gave her a hug and said, "Things will be fine." He watched his wife for a few moments, then said, "I really have to study, dear. I will see you at dinner."

The three Roosevelts often ate together. In the summers they went to the family camp on Campobello Island. They spent their weekends at Hyde Park, sailing, riding, and playing tennis. And the family grew rapidly. In 1906 Eleanor gave birth to Anna. In 1907 James was born. Eleanor and her mother-in-law were kept busy trying to raise the babies. Franklin's life was filled with books and work.

He studied hard for his classes at Columbia and also for the bar examination. If he could pass that test, he could be sworn in as a lawyer. Months before his graduation, he passed the bar. He dropped out of school and started practicing in one of the leading corporate law firms of New York City.

Like the other lawyers in his firm, he fought for more money for big companies. But it was the smaller cases that interested him more. These were about protecting people, and often poor ones. Franklin had to learn how to gain the trust of these clients. It took speaking—and listening—in a different way than with his wealthy friends. He couldn't use the same fancy words that impressed his professors or the smart-aleck humor his schoolmates had liked. His jokes were earthier now and he laughed louder. It worked— and it felt right to him.

He changed his tone when he defended these clients in court, too. Instead of the polite, serious arguments and fancy legal terms he used when fighting on behalf of a company, he argued passionately for these people. He still used every bit of his legal training and his brilliant mind, but now he spoke straight English and used humor. It worked. He loved these clients and the excitement of fighting for their causes.

That was the best part of his job. Most of his hours were spent in paperwork and researching in law books. Other young lawyers in the firm worked happily like this for years, knowing they would someday be earning a great deal of money. Money didn't really matter to Franklin. His father had left him a trust fund. It paid him regularly, simply for being Franklin Delano Roosevelt. Eleanor had an income like that too. Without even lifting a finger, they were wealthy, and would be for the rest of their lives.

Franklin's children had the very best of everything. When he had time to be home, they had a wonderful, warm, funny Daddy who would play with them endlessly. He ran races with them on his shoulders, hiked with them through the woods, and played chase games until everyone was exhausted. When Franklin was at work, Eleanor and Mother and a team of nannies cared for Anna and James.

In 1909 a newborn named Franklin Roosevelt Jr. died. There was nothing the doctors could do. "We just can't be expecting every child to survive, you know," they reminded the young couple. "But you'll have many more babies." Franklin was quiet about his loss while he consoled Eleanor. Soon she was pregnant again.

They visited cousin Teddy in the White House, went to parties, and spent time in their homes with Mother. Eleanor had her babies, her knitting, and her little circle of friends. Life had settled into a comfortable pattern.

Franklin's work was comfortable too. But comfort was not enough for Franklin. He remembered the wild thrill of the torchlight parade in honor of his cousin. Running for office in clubs at Harvard had been exciting too. Franklin thought about the joy of winning.

Cousin Teddy urged Franklin to enter politics. The president seemed to live a life of constant excitement. He traveled around the world. Theodore Roosevelt was on the front page of every newspaper in the country. Franklin often thought about his powerful cousin.

One day Franklin looked across his desk at the other young lawyer who shared his office. He picked up a pencil and tapped it on a pad of paper. The other lawyer glanced up.

"I'm not going to practice law forever, you know," Franklin said, almost talking to himself. "I think I'll run for office, the first chance I have."

His coworker, Grenville, looked at him. "Why would you want to do that?" he asked.

"Well"—Roosevelt paused, then admitted his dream out loud—"I want to be president. And"—his pencil drummed sharply on the desk—"I think I have a very real chance."

His Own Plan

At the Dutchess County Democrats' Picnic of 1910, Franklin listened to the bands, ate hot dogs with sauerkraut and clams, drank beer, and talked happily with everyone he could. He knew that he would be involved in this kind of politicking when he ran for office someday.

Toward evening someone asked him to make a speech. Franklin said yes, but he was nervous. This was something he had never tried before. He had lived his life in Hyde Park, and as a Democrat, but he didn't know how it would feel to speak out about the things he cared about. Franklin quickly thought over what was important to him: the land, the farms, fair pay and working conditions, clean, honest government. That was what was important to these people, too. He reminded himself not to speak like a lawyer, but like those clients he'd championed in the courtroom . . . like Teddy at the torchlight parade. Franklin swallowed his fear, took a deep breath, and put his heart into the speech.

". . . and I thank you." He had not even finished the words when applause erupted. Franklin felt a flush of warmth. His grin spread until it seemed his face would crack in two, and still the applause rolled on.

"Franklin!" One of the local Democratic organizers rushed to shake the twenty-eight-year-old's hand. "That was wonderful!" He pulled Franklin closer. "We want you to run for the state senate this year." The organizer turned to the crowd. "Don't we?" There were excited shouts. "What do you say?" he pressed Franklin.

"If anyone could win it, a Roosevelt could!" someone else yelled.

Franklin looked over the fairgrounds. He knew that the Democrats were up against a wealthy, well-known Republican senator that year. Most of the voters were Republican, too. The odds would be five to one against him winning. He knew his mother would say it was too soon to enter politics. She'd say he should choose a race where he could start out a winner. In the back of his mind Franklin saw Isaac Roosevelt's portrait hanging proudly on the wall in Hyde Park. STATE SENATOR it said.

The crowd started a chant, and Franklin felt his heartbeat race. "I'll do it!" he said, raising both arms. "And I'm going to *win* it!" The crowd cheered.

They cheered him everywhere in Dutchess

County. Most politicians ran quiet, intense races for office. Franklin rented a Maxwell touring car and spent four weeks driving to every town and village. In 1910 cars were still newfangled. They were expensive, uncommon, and most of them were painted black. Franklin's was cherry red.

Ten times a day he would stop and leap out of the convertible, looking rich, elegant, and thoroughly modern. Townspeople flocked to see, just out of curiosity. Franklin was careful to sound like the voters themselves. He spoke to the farmers and tradespeople about what *they* cared about—and they voted him into office.

That year many other Democrats were elected, including Woodrow Wilson as president. Theodore Roosevelt had served two terms, as many as the law allowed, so he retired. He told the press that he thought his nephew Franklin was a fine politician—even though he was a Democrat.

Franklin was aiming for the presidency, but he knew he needed a firm base of support in his own state. In the New York State Senate, he did not talk about national goals. He proposed a bill called "Protection of Lands, Forests, and Public Parks," and other bills that would help local agriculture and the poor people who lived in crowded cities. He believed in the laws he helped make, and they helped to make him popular.

Being popular wasn't enough though. Voters did not get to choose who would be the United States senator from New York. Instead, powerful politicians in the state government chose from among their friends who would run, and the legislature elected the winner. Most of these men lived in New York City, and they had earned the nickname "Tammany Hall," after their meeting place. They felt threatened by this rich young man with movie-star looks and an uncle who'd been in the White House. They complained about him being a spoiled, rich college boy and a toplofty snob. They got a photograph of him with his little glasses halfway down on his nose and his head tilted back and sent it to all the newspapers.

"It makes me look like an English duke," Franklin moaned. He went to work on himself again, the way he had when the boys teased him at Groton, changing how he dressed and spoke and stood, and even how he smiled.

When Tammany Hall announced who would run for senator, Franklin and his young friends in the state senate refused to simply obey the party "bosses." He made angry speeches and fought back against the hateful things the bosses said about him. Franklin made national news for going against the boss system, and it made him popular with voters everywhere. "I love a good fight," he told the newspapers.

Woodrow Wilson, the governor of New Jersey, was running for president. Franklin had heard the man's ideas and liked them, so he went for a visit. Wilson, a retired schoolmaster, reminded Franklin of Reverend Peabody with his strong moral character and firm ideas. Roosevelt told Wilson about his own experience sailing and piloting large motor boats in tricky tidal waters. They both agreed on the need for change in government. Franklin was so impressed that he offered to help campaign for Wilson.

That summer Franklin did not campaign for Wilson, or for himself, either. He lay in bed, sick with typhoid fever, wondering how he could run for the next term in the state senate. A friend named Louis Howe came to see him. Louis, a newspaperman, knew that voters liked tall, athletic, handsome candidates like Franklin. Howe had a sharp mind for politics, although he did not have the good looks that a politician needed.

Louis called Roosevelt "beloved and revered future president." Better still, he offered to run

Franklin's campaign for state senate until he was well again. Franklin agreed. He never did do any speeches that year. Howe got him reelected anyway, with letters, posters, and press handouts.

The Roosevelts had another son by now, Elliott, and a new rental house in Albany, near the state capitol building. Whenever Franklin could, he spent time playing wild games with the children, almost as if he were a child himself. Often, though, he didn't see his family for days.

The Roosevelts thought that would change when Woodrow Wilson was elected in 1912. Franklin knew that a new president gets to ask his friends and coworkers to take important jobs in his new government. Though illness had kept Franklin from campaigning, he had already worked hard for Wilson's nomination. He expected a big job offer that would use his talents. Wilson offered him the job of collector for the Port of the City of New York. Everyone in the state would know him. But Franklin wanted more. When Wilson offered him a post as assistant secretary of the navy, Franklin said yes. It was the same job that his cousin Teddy had held on his way to the presidency!

The Roosevelts moved yet again, to a home in Washington, D.C. Soon there was a new baby, another boy named Franklin Delano Roosevelt Jr. Less than two years later, baby John was born. Eleanor and Mother Roosevelt had their hands full with five children. Franklin was busy with work.

How he loved it! Franklin was in charge of seeing that things went smoothly between a hundred thousand people and the United States Navy that employed them. It meant he had to get to know hundreds of powerful people—and they had to know who he was. His life was a series of parties, trips to naval bases, and important meetings.

In 1914 war broke out in Europe. Franklin Roosevelt now became even more valuable

to the government. He spoke several languages. He had traveled throughout Europe since he was a child. He knew these countries, and he'd seen how their different societies worked. He now learned war secrets and details about horrible poison gases being used in the battle. He kept the frightening count of soldiers dying in the very fields he'd bicycled through as a child.

Franklin kept track of what was going on all over the United States, too. In 1916 there was a terrible outbreak of polio. Franklin knew the number of children sickened by this mysterious "infantile paralysis" epidemic, and he knew how many had died from it. Poliomyelitis was frightening because no one knew how it spread. There were no shots yet to protect people. Hundreds of children were sickened with polio every day in the cities. Worried parents made sure swimming pools were closed. Children were kept inside their homes, camps and clubs stopped meeting—but still the polio spread.

Once a child was infected, there was nothing the doctors could do but wait as the disease painfully destroyed nerves that control muscle activity. Over a few days, the child might lose the use of his legs. Or his legs and his arms. Or even the muscles that let him breathe.

If the patient survived, society was not kind to him. A "polio" seemed to vanish. The treatments were long and very painful and braces or crutches carried him through the rest of his life. Most "polios" went to grim sanitariums to live their lives as cripples, hidden away so "normal" people wouldn't have to see them in schools or on the street. "Normal" people were supposed to look— and act—perfect. If you couldn't, it was kept secret.

It was a nightmare to all parents, including the Roosevelts. Franklin was glad that the family was summering at Campobello Island, far from the cities where the epidemic was worst. He told them to stay there for their own safety. When fall came and the children had to go home for school, Franklin told them he would come and get them. But how?

Traveling south on a train, they might catch polio from other passengers. Driving through crowded cities was risky, too. To solve the problem, Franklin steered a huge ship belonging to the United States Navy to the little dock at Campobello. The whole family and their servants boarded. The children played with the sailors while their gallant papa showed off his seamanship as they steamed toward home. Instead of docking in Boston or New York City, Roosevelt had the ship sail straight up the Hudson River to Hyde Park. Servants carried the children on up to the house so their feet would not touch dirt that might carry polio.

As colder weather arrived, there were fewer new cases of polio in the country. By wintertime, the epidemic was over. The Roosevelts could relax about their children and return to their routine: Eleanor, Franklin's mother, and the staff of nannies and tutors were home raising the children.

Franklin was traveling more and more. Whenever he could, he took the helm of navy ships, chatting and joking with the sailors. He spent weeks away from his dear family. He wasn't lonely, for there were always parties and political events to attend in Washington. Men and women were drawn to his power and energy, so making friends was easy. One young woman named Lucy Mercer seemed to be at all the parties. She had great social connections and Eleanor hired her as a social secretary.

Franklin began to trust Lucy, and his friendship with her deepened. It seemed he had everything now: a big, happy family; a huge circle of friends; and a friend like Lucy, too. The excitement of it all made him feel alive, and it seemed his political career was right on track.

In 1916 Wilson ran for a second term as president. Franklin campaigned for him. The issues that year were simple. Battles between countries had always happened, but now violence had spread over Europe. So many countries were involved that, for the first time, it seemed to be a world war. The Germans had announced that they would send submarines to sink any ships in the sea. They were trying to starve out France and England so they could take them over. Roosevelt thought the United States should join the fight to protect its friends.

Wilson argued against it. He said they should see if things couldn't be settled by talking instead of by killing. Above all, he did not want to fight until war was forced on America by the Germans. "I want history," he said, "to show that we have tried every diplomatic means to stay out of war." Attacking first seemed morally wrong to him. He wanted "to come into the court of history with clean hands."

Roosevelt finally agreed, knowing that Wilson was right. But he looked through law books searching for ways that would help the navy become battle-ready without breaking any laws. In April of 1917 Wilson finally called for a declaration of war.

Roosevelt made sure the navy was involved in the war in every way possible. He helped create new naval training centers, sped contracts for wartime supplies through, and made sure that the North Sea was mined by navy ships so the German submarines could not slip through. For him personally, though, it was not enough. Roosevelt wanted to get into uniform and fight for his country. His cousin Teddy told him it would be politically good to be seen as a soldier. But there was no way for Franklin to get out of his job and into the navy. He was furious, but there was nothing he could do.

For her part, Eleanor was working endless hours at a Red Cross canteen in Washington, cooking for the sailors and soldiers who came through the city. For some it was their last taste of homemade food before they left for war. For others it was their first real meal off the battlefield. Eleanor knew her time was well spent. She shared with Franklin how the men seemed to be feeling about the war and the government—when she saw him.

Toward the end of the war, Franklin finally arrived at the European front—but it was for a military inspection, not a battle. Part of the trip was glamorous. He met with King George and the young Winston Churchill in England. He met with heads of state in Paris and Rome, too. But everywhere he went, Franklin saw the destruction in the beautiful cities he had loved as a child. There were endless new cemeteries full of dead soldiers and sailors. Franklin saw the broken bodies of servicemen in the hospitals. He saw the victims of gassings, their skin horribly scarred, their eyes blinded forever. What he saw left him hating the whole idea of war.

The newspapers were calling it the "War to End All Wars," for surely no one would ever fight again after seeing the results.

The armistice formally declaring peace was signed on November 11, 1918, at 11 A.M. Soon afterward, both Franklin and Eleanor traveled back to Europe with other government officials. Together they attended diplomatic parties. While Franklin was in meetings, Eleanor talked with the war's survivors. She heard things that Franklin had missed. Her insights were as helpful to Franklin then as they had been in college. They were, he knew, a great team.

On the ocean liner on the way back home, President Wilson called Franklin into his cabin to talk about the League of Nations, a new organization that would bring countries from around the world together to meet and discuss differences. Wilson wanted to make sure that this dreadful world war ended all wars by using international diplomacy. Roosevelt, staggered by what he had seen everywhere in Europe, agreed.

Back in Washington, people were already talking about Roosevelt as a possible president someday. The rounds of parties started again, and twenty-year-old Lucy Mercer was there to keep Franklin company whenever Eleanor was at one of the other Roosevelt homes with the family. Lucy was beautiful and bright and fun to be with.

Eleanor thought so too, until Franklin came home to New York with the flu. As he regained his strength, she offered to help him with his paperwork. In among his navy and diplomatic letters, she came across a pile of letters from Lucy to Franklin. They proved that Franklin had fallen in love—with Eleanor's own secretary!

✦ ✦ ✦ ✦

"Franklin," Eleanor said coldly, "come in here." She quietly closed the door behind him, and then spun about, the letters in hand. Franklin stood speechless. He had never meant for this to happen. The face of his dear, wonderful wife was tear-streaked and white with anger. He put his hand out and moved to comfort her.

She stepped back and pulled herself up to her full, graceful height. "I will give you a divorce," she said.

"Don't be a goose!" he answered, trying to take the horror out of the scene. It only made things worse. Eleanor erupted, saying all sorts of angry, hurtful things that Franklin knew to be true. He deserved it all. But he also knew that he and Eleanor *must* not divorce. The same society that insisted that only perfect bodies were fit to be seen on the streets, insisted that all marriages be perfect—and forever. If he and Eleanor divorced, he would never become president. The reason didn't matter. People simply would not vote for any-one whose marriage was a failure.

The arguments raged for days in the Roosevelt household. Eleanor was fighting for her pride and her broken heart. Franklin was fighting to save his lifelong dream of becoming president.

Even Mother Roosevelt got into the argument, for once taking Eleanor's side. "If you don't give up Lucy," she told her son, "you will never get another penny of Roosevelt money." But it was not about money.

Finally they hammered out a solution. They would pretend to have the perfect marriage, but they would only be political partners. They were fond of each other, but that was why this hurt so much. They enjoyed each other's minds and humor, but the trust was gone. "And," Eleanor decreed, "if I am to live this lie, you must never see Lucy again."

Franklin could not imagine losing his friendship with Lucy, but he did not bother to argue with Eleanor about it. This plan would work.

They appeared in public as husband and wife in the years following, while Franklin raced after his political goals. In 1920 Roosevelt wanted to run for governor of New York. That was the path Teddy had taken. But Al Smith, New York's governor, was popular and wanted to stay in office. Franklin didn't want to be just another senator in the U.S. Capitol. He wanted a national stage. When Governor James Cox of Ohio was nominated to run for president as a Democrat, Roosevelt agreed to run with him for vice president.

Cox was fighting Warren Harding for the office. Harding knew the country was bruised after the war. He promised to return to the "normalcy" of isolation. That meant staying out of international treaties and, especially, out of the League of Nations.

Roosevelt and Cox visited the White

House to talk to Woodrow Wilson about how best to fight the campaign. When Roosevelt entered the Oval Office, he stopped, horrified. He had known that the president was sick. He had even known it was a stroke and that Wilson was seriously ill. But seeing the president weak like this—sitting in a wheelchair—it was too dreadful! The country needed a strong man for their leader, and Wilson's left arm was paralyzed and covered with a fringed shawl. "Thank you," the president said slowly, carefully, "for coming."

Franklin could not answer. No one should be seen like this. Franklin looked at the ceiling, at the carpet, out the window—anywhere but at Wilson. At last he looked at Cox. His running mate's eyes were filled with tears of pity. The two men found their voices at last. They promised to fight for the league, then left quickly. The picture of the broken man in the Oval Office stayed with Franklin.

He rushed into the campaign with zest even

though he knew his team would probably lose. A loss by Cox would not make him look bad. And the campaigning nationwide would be good practice for him. Besides, it would let him meet thousands of voters and local politicians all around America. He toured in a railway car, making up to seven speeches a day. He learned what tones and gestures helped get his points across.

He learned what made people cheer, and it wasn't the league. No matter how often he explained how important it was for the United States to be one of the nations that would talk, not fight over problems, no one wanted to hear it. They were upset about postwar shortages at home, high prices, and strikes by the newly formed labor unions.

Roosevelt lost, as he knew he would. But he learned. He returned to private life, taking a job with a financial firm in New York City to wait for his next political race. He channeled his endless energy into founding new businesses and serving on councils and boards. Everyone was glad to have the young Roosevelt on board. Now he had time to vacation with his children. They were old enough to learn to sail with him, to ride races, and to challenge in endless tennis matches at Campobello. Except for the tension between him and Eleanor, things were perfect. He had the big, happy family he'd always wanted and was right on track for the future he expected. Once again, it seemed that nothing could stop Franklin Delano Roosevelt.

"Doctor! Doctor!"

"Ready to come about?" Franklin called to his crew. Anna, Elliott, and James knew exactly what to do. They grabbed lines and prepared to haul in the sails on the *Vireo*, the Roosevelts' twenty-four-foot boat.

"Hard a'lee!" the captain cried. He swung the tiller sharply to turn the boat and ducked as the great white sail swung over his head. One by one the children ducked, too, then straightened as the sail passed, pulling in their lines and laughing with joy.

Franklin hadn't been able to come out with

them to Campobello Island these last few years, but this summer he expected to spend several weeks with his family. He needed the rest. His businesses, boards, committees, and charity work had left him exhausted, but he was not about to complain. He hadn't complained about falling overboard the day before either. He'd made a great joke of it, splashing and playing, but the water had given him a strange chilly feeling that would not go away.

"Look, Papa!" Anna said, pointing. "Do you see the smoke over there?"

Franklin stood up and shaded his eyes. "Looks like a fire," he said. "We've got to stop it before the whole forest flames up!" He took a breath. "Ready? About!" he ordered again. They sailed the boat to the shore and tied it. Coughing in the smoky air, they began beating at the fire with evergreen branches. "My branch is smoking, Papa!" Elliot called.

"Wet it down! That will cool it off!" Franklin

shouted. After two hours the fire was out. It was late in the afternoon and Franklin took a look at his children, smeared with ashes and stinking of smoke. He laughed. "I'll race you to the swimming pond!" he shouted.

"But Papa!" Anna said. "That's two miles away!" But he had already jogged off into the forest. When they caught up to him, Franklin was paddling out into the pond, fully clothed, and splashing at them.

"This isn't refreshing," James said. "The pond is too shallow. The sun has made it feel like a warm bath."

"Then let's try the bay," Franklin said. He was feeling strange. "A saltwater dip will refresh us all!" The children laughed.

"Papa, we can't keep up with you!" Anna said. Franklin hiked with them over the ridge and swam in the icy Canadian water. Then they hiked home. For the first time in the day, Franklin was not at the head of the line. He trudged into the house and peeled off his wet clothes. Dressed again, and warmly, he settled down in his favorite chair by the fireplace to read the mail. The dog curled up by his feet and sighed happily. Franklin couldn't concentrate. He picked up a newspaper. For once it wasn't interesting. His back hurt. That wasn't unusual, but the chill seemed to have hold of his bones.

"I think," he said, "I should take my tired old back to bed for a nap before dinner." No one watched as he slowly climbed the stairs and walked to his room.

It was the last time Franklin Delano Roosevelt would ever walk on his own.

All night long Franklin lay shivering under piles of blankets. When he woke up in the morning he didn't even want to open his eyes. But the sun was shining through the window. The children would be awakening, and they would want to play! It was his summer to really have fun with them. Franklin threw back his covers, put his feet on the floor, and stood up. One of his knees let go, and he flapped his arms to keep his balance. He made himself stand straight. Then he took a step toward the sunny window. His knee buckled again. He told it to straighten, but his knee simply wouldn't work.

Franklin hopped around the bedroom, leaning against the wall, then the table, then the windowsill on the way to the bathroom. He didn't want to make a fuss, so he hopped back to the bed and called for the maid. "I'm down with a touch of the flu," he told her. "Tell the family I am perfectly fine, but I am staying in bed until I can shake it off."

She felt his forehead. "Mr. Roosevelt, you are burning with fever!" she said. She called for Eleanor. Mother Roosevelt came up to see, too. The thermometer said Franklin's temperature was 102 degrees.

During the day they brought him cool drinks. His children looked in on him, too, but Franklin was keeping a secret. Whenever everyone left the room, he kept testing his legs. His right knee got weaker all day long. His right hip started to feel—and act—like it was made of sponge, not bones. And it hurt! His skin hurt, too, everywhere, and his joints ached. By the time the sun set, his left knee was beginning to wobble as well.

The next morning, Franklin could not stand at all.

"Eleanor," he said with apology, "perhaps we should call a doctor?"

"This is indeed strange." The doctor stood by the bed, his hands in his pockets. "I can't imagine what would be wrong with you. It is probably just a heavy cold." He shook his head. "You've always been strong as a horse, Franklin. A few day's bed rest and you'll be fine."

By the end of the third day, practically all the muscles from Franklin's chest down were useless. Nothing he did would make them move. He couldn't wiggle his toes or raise his knees. He could barely wave his fingers at his own children when their frightened faces peeked in. He couldn't turn over. And he couldn't get away from the pain.

"Eleanor," he finally begged, "please lift the blankets off my legs. The weight of them is more than I can bear." But when she slid the blankets off, he gasped in pain. His face turned white. The feel of the cloth sliding over his skin was like hot knives raking over it. The breeze from the window was worse. Cool air burned like dry ice against his skin until he thought he would scream. "Perhaps," he managed to say, "you could make a tent over my feet and legs? Don't . . . ah . . . ow! . . . don't let the cloth touch me, please, please."

"Let me call another doctor," Eleanor said.

This doctor came by train from Bar Harbor, Maine, to the ferry. He hurried from the dock to the house and listened to all the symptoms, starting with the ache in Franklin's often achy back. "Hmmm," he said. He examined Franklin, trying not to cause more pain. "Hmmm," he said again. "I've never seen anything quite like it." He thought a bit more, then declared that there must have been a blood clot in Franklin's lower back that was blocking all the nerve messages down to his muscles—but was somehow letting all the pain messages come right through. "What you must do," he told the horrified Roosevelts, "is rub him, hard, all over, especially massaging his back and legs."

"But . . . ," Eleanor tried to say, but the doctor was looking at his watch.

"When did you say the last ferry left?" He glanced out the window. "Wouldn't want to miss the boat. Let me know how soon the treatment takes effect. Should be just a few days." And he hurried away.

Every one of those "few days" felt like an

eternity to Franklin—an eternity of pain. If the weight of a blanket hurt, a "heavy massage" was absolute torture for Franklin. As kind hands rubbed at his body, his nerves told him that his legs were being ripped off, that they were being chewed by rats, or that they'd had boiling oil poured over them. His sickened nerves were lying, of course, but the feelings were just as horrible as if they had been true.

Between "treatments," Franklin lay helplessly in a blanket tent with his knees propped up over pillows. He had plenty of time to think. What was wrong with his body? He was thoroughly frightened now. None of it made sense and nothing seemed to be getting better. It seemed like he was becoming paralyzed. It was almost like polio—but his mind shut down at the thought. He was too old for "infantile" paralysis. The fear hurt almost as much as his poor sick nerves.

He thought about what the future would

be like if he stayed paralyzed. He thought about his wife. He thought about his dear children. He thought about being a politician. All of it frightened him, but worst of all was the thought of fire. If he smelled smoke, what could he do? He imagined lying helpless in his bed and burning to death.

As the days passed, bruises began to form on his paralyzed body wherever it rested against the bed. These bedsores would only get worse if he didn't shift his weight off them. No matter how hard he tried, Franklin could not get his body to move. Eleanor had to turn him over several times each day. For Eleanor it was like turning over a big old mattress, but this "mattress" was covered with raw nerves. Franklin couldn't help. It was all he could do not to cry out in pain. Over and over again during the day, the women he loved had to come and hurt him worse.

And nothing they did seemed to be helping. Franklin lay waiting in horror for the next treatment. He could not go to the bathroom at all without help. He could not eat or drink without help. He could not dress or shave or brush his teeth without help. What would he do if there were a fire? He was trapped by this useless body, and he would burn alive. Every bit of help from his family made him want to scream in agony. He just wanted it all to be over so he could play with his children—so the pain would go away.

A few days later the Roosevelts got a note from the Bar Harbor doctor. He had changed his mind about what was causing Franklin's trouble. "A lesion," he thought now. And he said it might take a long time to heal. He enclosed a huge bill for his services.

Franklin ached—and he ached to be well again. When the pain let him think, he thought about the family. He thought about his next step on the way to the presidency. There were so many letters he should be writing to keep in touch with his political friends; his businesses needed attention; and he should be keeping up on the news, too. Mother Roosevelt was glad to read aloud to him, but he could not concentrate.

Eleanor had moved into the room with Franklin. Day and night she took care of his needs. When she had to leave for a nap or a break, Louis Howe came in to take over. When he had to take a break, Mother Roosevelt stepped in. The dogs quickly learned not to jump on the bed. Instead they lay on the bedroom rug nearby, guarding the sick man.

There was no break for Franklin. The endless pain gripped him day and night as he lay in the bed. Instead of getting better, his muscles were weakening further. He couldn't move his thumbs now. This clearly wasn't a "heavy cold." It wasn't acting like a "blood clot" either, or a "lesion."

Eleanor, Mother, and Louis Howe talked it over. Franklin was thirty-nine, but this surely looked to them like infantile paralysis. The

Roosevelt children were allowed only peeks at their father through the door in case it was polio, and in case polio could be spread through the air. The dogs lay on the carpet day in and day out, silent companions for their master. Ten days after Franklin had fallen ill, Eleanor sent for a doctor from Boston, a specialist in polio.

"Oh, dear!" the doctor cried when he heard about Franklin's treatment. "You must stop, and at once!"

The doctor examined Franklin and called Eleanor, Mother, and Louis to the parlor. He closed the door and asked them to sit down.

"It *is* polio, isn't it?" Eleanor said, her eyes full of tears.

"Yes. Franklin has polio, as you suspected. But you can only hurt a victim of polio with massage!"

Eleanor was horrified. "What can we do, then?" she begged.

"Nothing."

"What?!" Mother Roosevelt's voice was almost a shriek.

"Someday," the doctor predicted, "there may be a vaccine to prevent polio or a medicine to cure it. For now, there is nothing."

Mother dabbed at her eyes with a lace handkerchief.

"Polio destroys nerves," the doctor went on. "We don't know how to stop it. We can only wait to see how much paralysis he has. When the infection stage is over, well, then we'll see what can be done."

The family stood, stunned, silent. There wasn't much that was worse than polio, and they all knew it. And polio didn't go away, like other diseases. The paralysis lasted as long as the patient lived, *if* he survived the infection.

"You can feel lucky. It has not affected his heart, his swallowing, or his breathing," the doctor said. "He will survive. Probably."

"There . . . there is nothing?" Louis gasped.

"He has such plans. . . . He *had* such plans."

No one had to say a thing. If it really was polio, Franklin could never be president. He would always have to stay home, out of sight . . . a cripple.

"My baby!" Mother Roosevelt said. She put her hand over her mouth, then cleared her throat and spoke firmly. "I will keep him at Hyde Park. He will be comfortable there."

"But—," Eleanor began.

"Let's see how the disease runs before we go making plans," the doctor said. "Why don't you take him to the hospital in a month? I can leave painkillers for now that may help a bit. Hot baths will ease the agony, too." He looked at the family's stunned faces. "And someone must tell him."

Eleanor nodded.

"You should know," the doctor told her, "that adult polio victims can become terribly depressed when they get this news. The life they thought they had is over. It can take a

long time for them to even begin to understand what they have lost. It takes even
longer for them to find what they still have."

"Polio!" Franklin argued from his bed. "How
can it be? I'm too old for that. It can't be
polio!"

He refused to believe it, but the tears on
Eleanor's face told him the truth. So did his
symptoms. He'd read about polio all his life.
He knew—he *had known*—lying there day
after day. He had thought it might be polio.
But it couldn't be! His thoughts were all
jumbled. He wanted to shout *No!*, to throw
off the covers and run out the door. He
wanted to keep on running, running until his
legs burned, until his lungs exploded and he
left this nightmare behind him.

Under the covers, those legs lay limp.

"Franklin . . ." Eleanor reached to brush
her hand across his cheek.

Franklin winced. He couldn't help it. Her

touch meant only more pain. Eleanor pulled her hand back and wiped her own tears instead.

"May I be alone for a few moments?" Franklin managed to say.

When the door closed, Franklin lay helpless with his terror. He told himself he must be strong for his family. He told himself that it was unseemly to make a fuss. But his life was *over*! He kept his response—crying, cursing, sobbing, screaming, pleading, praying—silent. The children must not be disturbed. Louis, he thought, would think less of him if he knew. Mother would hear if he made a fuss.

But the grief kept pouring out. *My body!* he mourned. He wept, remembering running races with the children, leaping onto stages as crowds cheered, galloping on horseback, hiking to the hilltops to watch sunsets. It was over. All of it.

How could this happen? And to *him*, for heaven's sake? He was someone *special*. He always had been—everyone knew that. But instead of being the powerful young politician, he was a limp bundle of pain, forever helpless. His own body was diseased—it was the enemy—the betrayer of his dreams. Franklin lay, furious, trying not to make a fuss as his future died.

Over the next weeks Franklin's mind found a way to deal with the terrible news. He denied it. He refused to accept how serious the disease was and what it meant to be paralyzed. He would triumph over this somehow, he told himself. He would beat the polio. He was a Roosevelt, after all. And didn't he always say he loved a fight? That's all this was. Another fight—one he would win! He was young and strong and had the best medical help money could buy. He made plans, knowing he would be back on his feet soon. His friends would cover for him while this embarrassing period lasted. He had lots of friends. Roosevelt lay in bed planning his amazing triumph over a dread disease, and his run for the presidency.

Four weeks later Louis Howe figured out a way to get Franklin to a hospital in New York City. There had been no amazing triumph over polio for Franklin. Every one of his muscles was painfully cramped in a spasm, locking his legs, feet, and lower back in strange positions. This meant he couldn't be carried in a chair or wheeled off Campobello Island. His body had to be moved on a stretcher, and very carefully.

He was strapped on a canvas pallet and lowered with ropes out of the second-story bedroom where he'd spent a month of agony. He was carried downhill across the yard, then lowered down a cliff to the dock. There his stretcher was handed over to men in a small, rocking boat. This was as bad as the fire terrors Franklin had. He knew that if the

boat flipped, he could not swim. He would just sink helplessly to the bottom. He did not complain, though. Instead he teased the men all the way to the sardine dock on the mainland. Louis Howe had called for the press to meet him on the far side of the wharf, so they would be busy when Roosevelt was lifted, like a baby, up onto the dock.

No one saw the men lift his stretcher and set it on top of a baggage cart. They wheeled it over a bumpy stone road to the railroad tracks. Every jolt and wiggle tortured his raw nerves, but Franklin grinned through it all. The Roosevelt train cars were eased into place on the tracks. A window had been removed, and Franklin's stretcher was raised to the opening and slid into the car.

Eleanor let Louis know when her husband's twisted body was ready for the press to see.

"Hi, fellas!" He grinned at the reporters. They crowded around the special sleeping bed made up in the train car. Franklin held a cigarette holder between his teeth. "It's nothing," he told them. "The doctor says I will be just fine." It was a lie, but Franklin's smile looked real and his cigarette holder was tilted up to a cheery angle.

"Mr. Roosevelt was enjoying his cigarette and said he had a good appetite," the *New York World* reported the next day. "Although unable to sit up, he says he is feeling more comfortable."

The reporters had wanted to believe him. So they did.

Roosevelt did too.

"Doctor Roosevelt"

For six weeks Franklin lay in the hospital. His fevers came and went, but the pain inside of his muscles was endless as they tightened up, pulling at his joints. The staff worked his legs and feet, fighting the stiffening of his muscles. Forcing them to straighten hurt horribly, but Franklin knew that if he was ever to walk, it had to be done.

He struggled to sit up, but the muscles in his back stayed limp. He was fitted with a tight corset that held his trunk stiff. It let him sit, but he had to carefully balance himself upright with his arms. Slowly his skin began to feel normal again.

The hospital hung a trapeze over his bed. When he first arrived, Franklin could barely lift his hands to the bar overhead. Over the weeks, he worked his weakened arm muscles without mercy—and without complaint. The strength returned to his grip. That was a triumph for Franklin. A politician needed a good firm handshake.

But a politician also needed healthy legs, and nothing Franklin did could bring them back. Polio specialists showed him how to swing his dead legs over the edge of the bed and help himself into a wheelchair. At that time wheelchairs were enormous, bulky wicker contraptions. They would not go through doors. No one had yet thought to make laws that provided access to public places for the handicapped, so there were no ramps to wheel around stairs or over curbs.

Franklin struggled emotionally. Except for

never joining the Porcellian Club back at Harvard, he'd always gotten everything he wanted. Now Franklin couldn't even get up on his feet. He'd always been handsome and healthy, but now his legs were withering. His name had always counted for something, but polio didn't care who it paralyzed. Franklin had always known he would be president. Now he couldn't see any future at all. It was as if he was sailing a broken boat through a new sea without a chart. He struggled, steering between tiny, painful triumphs and waves of complete hopelessness. Through it all, Franklin pretended to be overflowing with good cheer, so the people around him would not be upset by his real feelings.

"You should just retire, come home, and live with me at Hyde Park," his mother pleaded.

"Yes, you're right," he agreed with a smile. Mother Roosevelt went home and happily made changes for him in the Hyde Park mansion.

"He needs the excitement of politics!" Louis Howe told Eleanor. Together they begged Franklin not to give up his dreams.

"Yes, you're right," he agreed with them, and grinned. They worked happily to keep him informed and connected.

"Papa, we need to see you!" The children sent loving messages.

"Yes, you're right," he agreed, laughing aloud and hugging everyone. He needed everyone's help to live, so he didn't want to upset anybody.

When he was released from the hospital, Franklin went to his New York City home so he could be near the hospital for more physical therapy. While snow fell in the streets outside, he played on the floor with the children, tickling them and laughing. He arm wrestled the boys and bear hugged the girls. He refused to see the tension in the house between his wife and mother and Louis and the children, and made them all help him with his exercises, whether they wanted to or not.

He was using braces now, great heavy steel rods from his waist to his ankles. They held his legs out straight, and could be swung into a sort of "step." Roosevelt spent endless hours practicing these steps. The braces chafed and bruised his body, and he had to lean on crutches or have help from his sons, but it was almost like walking.

Franklin had to rely on the people around him for everything now. He needed help to dress in the morning, to put on his braces, to go to the bathroom, to get up whenever he fell down, to pick up his glasses if he dropped them, and to go to bed at night. His pride crumbled. He'd always had maids and nannies to help him, secretaries and cooks to do his work, but this was different. Now he couldn't survive without help—lots of it.

Outwardly he was cheery, but inside his mind was wild. He could not deny that his legs were paralyzed, but he refused to admit it to anyone. The physical therapists at the hospital loved the jolly man, but they worried secretly. Was he pushing himself too hard to "get over" his polio? It was all he ever did now, exercising morning to night as long as he could. He drove the family as hard as he drove himself and everyone was tired.

Franklin caught a cold that winter. Getting sick, he lost almost all of the progress he'd made since the polio attack. It was a terrible time for Franklin. He had to admit that his body was in charge, not his own willpower. He had to face the fact that all of his wealth made no difference. He was suffering just the same as the polio victims who had no money or status. Some of them were even making more progress than he was. It was there in front of his face daily: He was upper class, private-school and Harvard educated, and a *Roosevelt*—but there was really no difference between him and the rest of the world. Sweating and struggling alongside other polios, he had to admit that they were all the same.

It changed who he was. No more did he see himself as "above" the poor or "better than" the uneducated. He couldn't. They were his equals here in therapy. No longer could a crowd ever just be "votes." They were individuals—people with real troubles and true courage. He would never forget the lesson.

When summer came, Franklin took a vacation. His family also got a vacation, from the endless care of Franklin. Only Missy LeHand, his secretary, came along on a long cruise aboard a houseboat in the slow, steamy rivers of Florida.

Nearly alone, Franklin could take all morning to pull himself together emotionally. In the afternoons he worked his muscles as the therapists had taught him. The hot tropical air helped his muscles to relax, and Missy was a calming influence. She was young and strong, placid and kind. She worked as his nurse, as his therapist, and as his secretary, too, reading and responding to his mail. Best of all, she was a good friend.

Swimming in the warm Florida waters also helped. Roosevelt set about trying everything anyone claimed would help polio victims. He threw himself into each new therapy, stopping those that didn't work and continuing those that did. And always he told everyone he would be walking soon. "Two years"—he gave himself the goal—"no braces, no canes, or crutches."

"Roosevelt to be walking soon" the newspapers reported. It was too good to be true—a polio victim who would overcome the disease. They didn't see the struggle as, every day for years, Franklin took his crutches out and tried to walk down the driveway at Hyde Park. "I must get down the driveway," he would chant, his face gray with pain and dripping with sweat. "Just to the end of the driveway." He never made it.

For years the struggle went on as Roosevelt

thought only about his cure. He tried massage again, saltwater baths, ultraviolet lights, and even electric currents. He swung his legs, "walking" in the air while he held himself up on parallel bars with his arms. He wrote letters to doctors all over the world, asking about polio. They taught him what they knew and Roosevelt became an expert in his own disease.

With Missy's help he wove a community of specialists he could call on with questions. It was like the old days when he was carefully creating a network of political contacts. It felt good. Better still, it felt normal. Franklin had found a natural talent that had not been paralyzed by his disease. His mood began to change. Now his smiles were more real. *Here* was a reason to go on living. He would help find a cure for polio!

Most therapy for polios at that time was grim and painful. Hospitals for "cripples" were gray places, cheerless and dreary, and people spent years and years there. They were taught "skills" that were little more than nursery school crafts. The doctors did not expect them to ever go to work again or have a family. Nobody did.

Franklin's mind did not work that way. He might get discouraged sometimes, but underneath, he was an optimist. That meant that he could always find reasons for hope and good cheer. In Georgia, he found both.

The water seeping out from under Pine Mountain at Warm Springs, Georgia, is always bathwater hot. It is also heavy with minerals dissolved out of the rocks. People had long known about how good it felt to bathe in the water. A big old hotel stood by some pools filled with spring water. Little cabins had been built in the woods nearby, too. The place was run down and out of fashion. Few wealthy people vacationed there anymore. Several polios had discovered it and were amazed by the results. A friend wrote to Roosevelt, suggesting he might want to visit Warm Springs.

When Roosevelt swam in one of the pools at the old resort, he felt better right away. He was not cured, of course, but the heaviness of the mineral water made his body feel light. The hot soaking relaxed his muscles as he floated almost free of the pull of gravity. The feeling came back in his toes and he could walk around in the water. In the pools, he could do exercise therapy for two full hours before he was exhausted.

Franklin was thrilled. Missy and Eleanor had come along on the trip. They were not impressed by the shabby old buildings, but Franklin could not stop grinning. The farmers of the little town had been so friendly, following him as he got off the train from Atlanta, eighty miles to the north. Franklin felt he could understand these people. They were dirt poor, but they loved the land, just as he did.

The hot southern air felt good, and the hot-water pool was heaven! Franklin met a polio there who had exercised in the springs and learned to walk using canes. Franklin rented a cabin right away from Mr. Loyless, the owner. The place had no electricity or running water, daylight showed through cracks in the walls, and the furniture was old, but Franklin didn't care. He could swim there every morning and bask in the hot Georgia sun every afternoon. He was already planning how much sooner he would be walking. Eleanor went back home to tend to her husband's political life and his children.

Missy and Franklin decided to stay for months. A reporter from the *Atlanta Journal* heard about the famous Franklin Roosevelt's visit to the old resort. He spent days there, swimming with Roosevelt, sunning and watching the exercises, eating hot dogs from a cook shack near the pool, and taking notes.

When his article was printed, it bubbled

with all of Roosevelt's optimism. It talked about how polios had long found comfort in water, heat, and sunshine, and how Roosevelt was enjoying all three. It quoted doctors and therapists agreeing with the treatments. The article was reprinted in magazines all around the country.

Polios read it. Most could only dream of a place to go where they could relax and play cards with other polios, healing amid laughter instead of sighs. Many made plans to visit Warm Springs someday, others went right out and bought train tickets.

"Mr. Loyless," a messenger panted a few days later, "two people have just been carried off the train down at the station. What shall we do with them? Neither of them can walk."

Roosevelt and Loyless decided to ask townspeople to put the polios up for a few days while they fixed a cabin for them, widening the doors and putting in toilets and ramps. Before the cabin was ready, eight new polios had arrived. "What do we do?" Loyless said. "We need medical permits, therapists and contractors, more cooks, and . . ."

Roosevelt grinned. His quick mind was already thinking of ways to solve the problems. From his years as assistant secretary of the navy, he knew how to organize thousands of people and millions of dollars worth of material. Franklin's laugh rang out. He had found another talent the polio had not paralyzed.

Over the next few months the Meriwether Inn was transformed. Roosevelt had tables built into the pools to permit exercising in the water, a system of walkways paved with cement for wheelchair strolls, cabins rebuilt, and the main inn upgraded. When Mr. Loyless became ill in 1926, Franklin bought the entire resort. It cost him almost two hundred thousand dollars, two-thirds of all the Roosevelt wealth. Eleanor was thrilled to hear the old energy back in Franklin's voice,

but she was worried. "How will we pay for the children's education?" she asked.

"Mother will take care of them," he answered smoothly.

That easygoing confidence kept the treatment center growing. Roosevelt used all his people skills to gather medical support and financial funding. Franklin's cheer colored every bit of the treatment, too. There were games in the pool and contests, nicknames and laughter, hugs and encouragement. The polios teased their "Doctor Roosevelt" and he always responded with a playful grin.

He got a car for himself and had it rebuilt with hand controls instead of foot pedals. Franklin bought a farm for himself, too, with cows and chickens and fruit trees. Just as he had with his polio, he tried all sorts of modern farming ideas until he found ones that worked just right in the hot Georgia climate. He shared what he learned with other farmers. He would drive about, visiting his farm, exploring the countryside, and stopping in the town. He loved to talk to the local people and now he felt stirrings of the old political plans. Driving around in the car, he wasn't paralyzed. He listened to the poor farmers and their troubles. They had no electricity. No running water. No jobs. No money. No hope. Franklin imagined solutions to their problems—things he could change, if he were back in the government.

Back home, Eleanor and Louis were thrilled that Franklin was thinking about returning to public life. They talked Al Smith, the governor of New York, into letting Franklin give the speech nominating him for president at the party's national convention. It meant that Franklin would have to stand up before thousands of important politicians at the Democratic Convention in Madison Square Garden in New York City. Could he do it? What if he fell over? It was a risk for Al Smith, too. In the 1920s people were still turned off by anyone with a disability. But if Roosevelt could prove himself healthy and strong, he could jump back into politics.

Franklin and his son James practiced for months before the convention. "We can't let them see me in a wheelchair," Franklin said, "or being carried." He had been wearing his braces outside his pants in Georgia, where the polios were used to seeing hardware on one another. Now he wore them inside his pants, and the rods at the bottom were painted black so they would blend into his socks. These braces—and Franklin's legs tied inside them—had only two positions: straight out or bent to sit down.

He "walked" stiff-legged, swinging his heavy braces between crutches. It looked more natural if he gripped his son's arm. Either way, it was slow. It hurt. It was risky, too, but it looked like walking, and that was what mattered.

Roosevelt practiced the speech Al Smith had given him, until it sounded great—even the final quote about "the happy warrior."

The convention was a week long. Every day James took his father to Madison Square Garden long before anyone else arrived. Franklin was posed, sitting in a big chair, and there he had to stay until everyone left at the end of the day. To change position, James had to unlock his father's braces at the knees. That would draw attention to the very thing they wanted to keep secret. The delegates said they were glad he was back, but they hadn't seen him move yet.

Franklin was ready at the back of the platform when it was time to give his speech. James carefully handed him a crutch and stood back. In the balcony Eleanor began knitting furiously, putting all her worries into the movement. There was applause when Franklin was introduced, then a hushed silence. It was no secret that he had come

116

down with polio. It was a miracle he was here at all. Could he really walk? No one breathed.

Slowly Franklin shifted one crutch forward. He swung one leg up, struggling to keep his balance. Then he moved the other crutch forward. And took another step. James followed close behind, in case his father fell over backward. If he fell forward there would be no one to catch him. Franklin kept "walking," as everyone's eyes followed. It was only the length of a school bus, but it seemed to take forever to cross the stage.

At last he grabbed both sides of the podium. Franklin threw his head back in triumph and grinned widely—and the crowd went wild. They clapped and cheered until he motioned finally for silence. He gave Al Smith's speech beautifully, like the practiced politician he was. With the last words, the hall filled with a roar as people gave voice to their admiration, not for Al Smith, but for the bravery of Franklin Roosevelt. For an hour and fifteen minutes, they stamped their feet, they shouted his name, they clapped and hooted with joy at the victory.

Four years later, Al Smith wanted to enlist Roosevelt's support again. This time he was asking a tricky favor. "Will you run for governor of New York? That would free me up to make a real run at the presidency," he explained.

"But what if you lose the election?" Roosevelt asked. "You know that the odds are against the Democrats winning this year. You couldn't just go back to being governor."

"If I lose, you'll be there, standing in for me as governor," Al Smith told him. "You wouldn't have to do anything, of course. And you could spend as much time down in Warm Springs as you wanted. My friends could take care of the day-to-day work of being governor." It was clear that Smith wanted to run the show either way. Franklin's mind was whirling along. Teddy had been governor of New York before he was president. But Teddy hadn't been pretending—and neither would Franklin.

Roosevelt said he wasn't interested. Smith kept asking. Franklin said that he was needed to run Warm Springs. But Al Smith couldn't think of anyone else who would pretend to be governor so he kept calling Roosevelt. Franklin argued that he wasn't strong enough yet for a political campaign. It had only been seven years since the attack. He thought he'd really be walking in another two years or so.

Eleanor and Louis urged him to say no. They thought that since the Democrats were not likely to win the presidency that year, Franklin would probably lose, too. It would be a bad way to stage a comeback.

Al Smith kept calling and sending telegrams. He had his friends pressure Roosevelt, too. It didn't seem that anything would change Franklin's mind. Finally Al Smith got a very rich friend to pledge $100,000 to Warm Springs. He agreed to help in future fund-raising, too. "Franklin, this will help the folks in Georgia while you are out campaigning," Al Smith said.

Franklin cleared his throat. The Warm Springs Foundation could surely use the money. But he still didn't say yes.

"What if the party members put your name up and vote you in as their candidate?" Al Smith asked. "Would you refuse to lead?"

Roosevelt just grinned. Smith didn't need to hear an answer to know what Franklin was thinking. *Of course* he would lead, if asked by the voters . . . *if* he won the election . . . and he *would* win! The thought of the fight ahead stirred him as nothing else had for years.

Roosevelt knew that he would never let Al Smith make all the decisions. Franklin was already thinking about how he would use his power when he won the election for governor. Paralyzed or not, Franklin Delano Roosevelt was back on the path to the presidency!

Governor Roosevelt

"It is rare good fun to be back in action," Franklin told a friend as his campaign got under way. "I had almost forgotten the thrill of it." The Democrats had asked him to be their candidate for governor of New York, and Roosevelt had thrown himself into the fight gleefully.

An insulting editorial in the *New York Post* set the tone for his campaign. "Pathetic," they called his candidacy. They said Al Smith was "pitiless" for suggesting that the poor cripple could run for office. Other papers wrote that

Eleanor would have to do all his campaigning for him. They guessed he would only give four or five speeches in the month-long campaign and that he would resign and let someone healthy be governor if he did get elected.

Franklin decided to prove them all wrong. He gave more speeches in more places than any candidate ever had before. He toured New York State in an open car with a bar mounted in the back seat. When the driver pulled the car in front of a crowded stadium or hayfield, Franklin pulled himself up until his leg braces locked into their standing position. Roosevelt looked so positive and sure of himself that people couldn't help but cheer. He gripped his cigarette holder in his teeth at a jaunty, upright angle and wore a great, swooping cape over his suit and a dapper hat, too.

He would list all the towns he'd already visited that day and ask the crowd to judge his health for themselves. "Too bad about this unfortunate sick man, isn't it?" his strong

tenor voice rang out, teasing them all. The crowds always laughed with him.

Under his grin, Franklin hid suffering. The braces hurt. He was exhausted. Often the speeches were scheduled in upstairs meeting halls. Roosevelt had to be carried up like a baby, out of sight of the crowd. Once he had to be hauled up a fire escape and handed in through a window to get to the stage where he was to talk. Throughout the campaign he never let any of the embarrassment or discomfort show in his face or change his firm, jolly voice.

The day of the election, things went badly for Al Smith. As expected, he lost his bid for the presidency. By lunchtime it was clear that Herbert Hoover had won. The governor's race was different. At midday it was too close to call. At sundown it was still too close to tell if Franklin had won. It wasn't until long after midnight that the final returns were counted. The race had been incredibly close, but

Roosevelt had won. He teased about being the "one-and-a-half-percent" governor. The margin was tiny, but it made him a one-hundred-percent winner, the way he liked it.

On January 1, 1929 Franklin's hand rested on the old Dutch Bible from Hyde Park as he was sworn into office, repeating the same ceremony he'd watched thirty years earlier when his cousin Theodore Roosevelt had become governor.

Franklin settled right in, making it clear to Al Smith that he didn't need any help. "I've got to be governor of the state of New York, and I've got to be it *myself*," he told Frances Perkins, a longtime political ally. "If I weren't, and if I didn't do it myself, something would be wrong."

"I am not Teddy," he had often said on campaign. He needed to make his own mark more than ever now. He was planning on running for the presidency in four short years.

He needed voters all over the country to know—and like—him.

He believed that the government could help people. Franklin hadn't just talked during all those miles of campaigning. He'd listened, too, and he knew what people needed. He pushed for unemployment insurance to give laid-off workers money to live on while they looked for new jobs. To get electricity to poor, rural New Yorkers, he pushed for the state to build hydroelectric dams. He urged the state senate and house to give more money to the parks, the schools, and the hospitals, too. For people who'd been hurt on the job and old people, he tried to get programs going that would give them money to live on. He also tried to get laws passed protecting the rights of the disabled. It should be the state's duty to "restore to useful activity those children and adults who have the misfortune to be crippled," he argued.

Franklin quickly made changes in the

governor's mansion in Albany to meet his own physical needs. He added a swimming pool in the backyard for therapy sessions. The halls were widened for his wheelchair, and an elevator was installed. Ramps were placed over stairs. Two special "bodyguards" were hired to serve the new governor. Tall and strong, their job was to walk alongside Franklin while he leaned on their thick, muscular arms. Gus, a New York City policeman, and Earle, a state trooper, knew how to lift Franklin smoothly in and out of cars. When they came to a staircase, Gus would take one of Franklin's elbows and Earle, the other, and both would lift. It looked like the governor was climbing up the stairs, though his feet never touched the ground.

Franklin's entire schedule was planned around his disability, too. He stayed in bed until midmorning. He ate breakfast there, took phone calls, read papers and worked with his secretary, Missy, on letters. Midday he was in his office. He had lunch there at his desk, working on papers and holding meetings. In the afternoon he had physical therapy and a quick nap. Then it was the dinner hour. Roosevelt wanted crowds of people at the governor's mansion for meals. Lively conversation with a variety of viewpoints was important at home, since Franklin could not get out to meet other people at restaurants, theaters, or parties.

Besides Eleanor, Mother Roosevelt, and the children, the "family" table in Albany now included Louis Howe, Gus and Earle, Missy, and a string of reporters, legislators, and other visitors that was never the same two nights in a row. Eleanor was working with a school in New York City, so she was in Albany only part of every week. When she returned, she reported to Franklin on the conditions she'd seen at hospitals and factories, schools and boatyards. She became his eyes and ears away from home, while the steady stream of people came to the mansion. Anna, now married, came to visit with the Roosevelt grandchildren and their dogs. The boys were at school at Groton much of the time and brought their friends home. Summer weeks were spent in Campobello. There were frequent trips to Hyde Park. And Franklin always spent time in the spring and in the fall at Warm Springs.

He loved the endless confusion and excitement of life in Albany. He felt wonderful being able to help people. Fighting to get his way with the legislature was a zest-filled challenge. As a governor, he glowed with immense joy.

Almost a year after Franklin took office, on October 24, 1929, stock prices began falling so drastically that the day was called "Black Thursday." President Herbert Hoover tried to tell the country the problem was only temporary, but things just got worse. For weeks the market fell further and further. Businesses closed. Banks that had loaned them money had to close. First thousands, then millions of people lost their jobs. They couldn't afford to buy new things, so factories closed. People couldn't afford food, so farmers didn't make money either. The economy kept spiraling downward, and people became fearful about the future. They—and the economy—had entered a depression, the greatest the country had ever seen.

This meant that there was not enough money to make all of Roosevelt's great ideas happen in his state. Many of his plans were put on hold until the hard times passed, but things just got worse. Prices fell and fell. A hot dog cost a dime. So did a loaf of bread or a cup of coffee. But a lot of people didn't even have that much money. "Brother, Can You Spare a Dime?" was a popular song around the country. Millions went homeless in the cities. People lined up for blocks for the free lunches given out by charitable organizations.

In the Midwest a terrible drought had changed lush farm fields into dust bowls. Farmers could not grow crops to sell or to feed themselves. They could not pay their bills, either. Millions of them were homeless in the countryside, living in their cars, driving from place to place looking for work.

When Roosevelt ran for his second term in office in 1930, the campaign had a different feel. Now when his car drove around the state, the crowds didn't just want to hear him talk. They wanted to tell him how bad things were. At every stop he got an earful of the problems facing the voters.

President Hoover thought that helping the poor would make them lazy. He gave money to businesses, insurance companies, railroads, and banks instead. He thought the money would "trickle down" from the rich bankers and businessmen to the poor.

The people who crowded around Roosevelt's car were desperate. They had lost their jobs and were scared that their families would starve. They were the ones who needed help, and Franklin could see that. These people weren't lazy. They *wanted* to work, but in this economy, they were helpless.

Roosevelt knew all about being helpless. He understood the anger and frustration and hurt pride of these good people. *His* people. He promised to help them if he was elected to a second term as governor.

Once again his political opponents said he was too weak and crippled for the job. Roosevelt went to insurance companies and asked them to figure out how bad a risk his health really was. They had a panel of doctors examine him. Twenty-two companies agreed to sell him insurance policies, proving that they were willing to bet their scarce money that he was strong and healthy—and would stay that way. His campaign workers made sure that copies of the insurance reports went to every newspaper in the state.

In 1930 he won reelection and went to work finding solutions to the problems of the depression. As he had with his own polio, he called in experts so he could learn everything possible about the economy. And he began testing ideas that seemed sensible, trying one idea after another.

One of his plans, the Temporary Emergency Relief Administration, or TERA, made a difference for millions of New York State families. It put people to work by making jobs for them—jobs keeping parks, creating roads or public buildings, managing land and the environment. For those who still could not find jobs, TERA helped with housing, food, and clothing. To pay for the TERA programs, he had to double the income tax. His opponents screamed that it would be the ruin of New York State. Instead, it was the helping hand that countless families needed to get them through the Great Depression.

The United States was not alone in its economic troubles. Many countries around the world were struggling with economic depression. People everywhere were poor and hungry and desperate. Their countries seemed to be doomed. They looked to strong leaders for help. In Germany young Adolph Hitler fed on their fears and gave them hope. He talked about creating a Nazi Third Reich that would last a thousand years. Many people followed him. They talked about making him chancellor and starting his "New World Order" soon.

There were so many problems here in the United States that hardly anyone was paying attention to the rest of the world. Herbert Hoover's plans weren't working at all to stop the depression. Instead it was getting worse. The economy seemed broken; the whole country, crippled.

"Doctor New Deal"

"The candidate," *Time* magazine told the nation, "while mentally qualified for the presidency, is utterly unfit physically." All the extra effort—and pain—that Franklin had poured into being governor didn't matter when people read statements like that. Now that he was running for president, he had to prove himself all over again, to the press and to the voters.

His campaign staff contacted a famous Republican writer. They asked Earle Looker to investigate Roosevelt and write an article for *Liberty Magazine*. Looker asked the American Medical Association to choose three doctors to examine Franklin. They, like the insurance company doctors, gave him a clean bill of health. The writer followed Roosevelt around for days, watching him work. Looker was exhausted, but Franklin's endless energy and cheer had never drooped.

"I have come to the conclusion," Looker wrote about forty-nine-year-old Franklin, "that he seemed able to take more punishment than many men ten years younger. Merely his legs were not much good to him." Copies of the article were sent to every Democratic Party county chairman in the entire country, to reporters and writers, newspapers and politicians. It helped to calm people's worries, though it didn't stop all the rumors. Next Franklin set about making his campaign as public, modern, exciting—and active—as possible.

When the Democratic Convention in

Chicago nominated him to be their candidate for president, he didn't just phone his acceptance to them. That was what people expected. Instead, the whole Roosevelt family flew to Chicago so Franklin could accept in person, standing tall in front of everyone.

Flying was still new. Few airlines had scheduled flights. Most Americans had never flown, and never expected to. The Roosevelts squeezed into a cramped Ford Trimotor plane. The flight from Albany to Chicago bounced through a series of windy thunderstorms. The children were airsick, but Franklin was thrilled by the wild ride. When he was helped out of the door, reporters and cameras awaited him.

The flight was news. A personal acceptance speech was news, too, and the press was ready to report every detail. They recorded his great, infectious grin and sparkling eyes for the world to see. That was just what Franklin wanted. He had decided that what

America needed most, with its poor crippled economy, was what all of the polios had needed at Warm Springs—a positive attitude and an energetic search for solutions. He intended to lead the country in both.

His speech was carried by radio. That had never been done before either. Most homes that had electricity had a radio in their living room, and people gathered around to listen. This evening they all heard Roosevelt.

"I pledge you"—his voice rang out—"I pledge myself, to a new deal for the American people. . . . Give me your help, not to win votes alone, but to win in this crusade to restore America to its own people!" He listed all the programs he intended to use to heal the sick economy: regulating the stock market, making jobs through public works programs, reforestation of damaged lands, help for poor farmers and home owners, letting people buy and sell alcoholic beverages, and a handful of other ideas. Everyone could find something to like in the list—and find some hope, too. The crowd was cheering long before his speech ended.

The next day a political cartoon appeared in a prominent newspaper showing a poor farmer in his empty field, looking up at a plane sweeping across the sky. On the plane were the words "New Deal." Other writers began calling him "Doctor New Deal," since he seemed to know what to do to heal the ailing economy.

Within a week Roosevelt, too, was sweeping across the country on a whistle-stop campaign. Instead of just giving a few radio speeches, as people expected, he boarded a train and rode it into their town. Papers and radios told them when to expect Roosevelt and a train whistle would blow to get their attention. When crowds came running, Franklin stepped from his special car out onto a platform, clinging to his son James's arm. His big grin, great hope, and enthusiasm touched everyone. He introduced the crowd to members of his family and to the solutions he hoped to put to work the moment he was elected. A few moments later, the train pulled out of town, followed by the cheers of the crowd.

At night Roosevelt held open houses, welcoming local politicians and townspeople into his train. There he kept a lively discussion going until after midnight. The next morning he did it all again.

On election night he was home in Hyde Park. He was unusually quiet as the results came in, thinking about the incredible responsibility he was taking on—leading a country of millions of people through a Great Depression. When it was clear he had won, and by a landslide, his sons helped him out onto the front porch. A huge torchlight parade had come from town to cheer. And cheer they did as, grinning, he announced his win.

Late that night James went upstairs with

his father. He took Franklin's braces off and stood them in the corner. Then he helped him change into pajamas. Franklin looked down at his lifeless legs. "All my life I have been afraid of only one thing," he told his son. "Fire. Tonight I think I am afraid of something else."

"What?" James helped his father shift into bed. Then he pulled the blanket up.

"I'm afraid I may not have the strength to do this job."

By the next morning his doubts were hidden away again, and he dove into work as president-elect.

With his inauguration still several weeks away, Franklin had time to travel as he made his plans and gathered key people around him for the term ahead. It was February and he was in Miami, Florida, with the mayor of Chicago. A crowd gathered as his open car stopped in the street. He grinned, stood up, and gave a quick speech. The crowd cheered and he sat back down by Mayor Cermak.

Suddenly shots rang out. Roosevelt faced his attacker as the man fired five bullets at him. His aim was bad. Franklin was not hit, but several bystanders fell to the pavement screaming. Mayor Cermak stood up. A bullet slammed into him and he fell from the car.

"Go!" the Secret Service man screamed at Roosevelt's driver. "Get out of here!"

"No," Roosevelt said. When the car moved ahead, he commanded. "Stop! We're going back for the mayor!"

The driver backed up and Roosevelt insisted that Cermak be lifted into the seat beside him. "To the hospital!" he roared, feeling for the man's pulse. "Hurry!"

"Tony," he cradled the dying man close, trying to comfort him. "Keep quiet, don't move. It won't hurt if you keep quiet."

Franklin waited in the hospital as doctors fought to save Cermak. He spoke with the other victims, too, and with Cermak's family when they arrived. Those bullets had been meant for him, he knew, and he wasn't even president yet. Newspapers everywhere praised his bold actions and kind words. They reported his incredible courage, facing the gunman. They wondered if he even knew what fear was.

On March 4, 1932, millions of Americans gathered around their radios again to hear what fifty-one-year-old Roosevelt would say as he laid his hand on the old Bible and took the presidential oath. The depression had only gotten worse since he'd been elected. The government itself had run out of money and people were truly losing hope.

"The only thing we have to fear," he told them firmly, "is fear itself." He outlined a plan with dozens of parts, each designed to help get the country back on its feet. He sounded sure each would work, too. He asked for "broad executive power to wage a war against the emergency, as great as the power that would be given to me if we were, in fact, invaded by a foreign foe."

He took that power and immediately closed every bank in the country for a few days. Only those that were well run were allowed to again open. They got a new special backing from the government to cover every penny of their investors' money, the by a Federal Deposit Insurance Corporation.

To carry out the rest of his plans, Roosevelt needed friends—lots of them. Even if he asks for extra powers, no president of the United States is ever all-powerful. He cannot make laws. The Constitution says he is only one of three branches of the government—the executive branch.

Lawmaking is up to the Senate and House of Representatives—the legislative branch. The senators and representatives there are elected by voters. Like the president, they have to listen to what the people say or they will be voted out of office.

The third branch—the judicial—is topped by the Supreme Court, which decides whether laws are constitutional. The justices there are nominated by the president, but must be voted on by the Congress. Once they are appointed, they stay there for life, so they never have to worry about pleasing voters, only about protecting the Constitution.

Other countries do not have such a safe system to control their leaders. In Germany Adolph Hitler had been sworn in as chancellor. When he announced he wanted extra powers to fight the depression there, nothing kept him from taking them. When he said he was going to increase the glory of Germany and the German people by force, nothing stood in his way.

For Roosevelt, having friends among the press and in the voting public would make it easier to get Congress to pass the laws he needed to put his plans to work. He could worry about the Supreme Court later. Roosevelt began holding a new kind of press conference. Other presidents had made reporters hand in their questions in writing. Later, in a formal pressroom, these presidents answered only the questions they wanted to, with answers that were practiced and polished ahead of time.

Now Roosevelt just threw open the doors of the Oval Office at the White House. Reporters and photographers crowded in, sitting on the floor when all the chairs were taken, or standing against the wall. Roosevelt made it seem like a party, laughing and grinning and cracking jokes with them. He answered any question they asked, and remembered their names and even their children's names. He told them secrets, too, trusting them not to print them. It was like having a good friend in the White House. When Franklin asked them a favor—"No movies of me getting out of the backseat, boys"—they were happy to agree. After that, it was rare to see pictures of him in his wheelchair or at an awkward moment.

Most of the reporters just set their cameras down while he was being carried. They policed themselves too, standing in the way of any photographer who was snapping an unflattering shot. The Secret Service was known to grab a camera and pull its film out when cruel pictures were taken. It was important that the country believe that Roosevelt was the strong leader it needed to get through the crisis.

Eleanor also used the press, holding her own press conferences. They were limited to women writers and reporters, professionals who seldom had a chance to talk to major political figures. She also wrote a weekly newspaper column sharing what she had seen in her tours of the country.

Her husband was an expert at using the

radio to make friends with the American people. Everyone gathered by their radios to hear great singers like Eddie Cantor. They listened breathlessly to adventures of *The Lone Ranger* or *The Shadow*, and they laughed with *Amos 'n' Andy*. In New York, Governor Roosevelt's "fireside chats" had been broadcast over the radio, too. In each "chat" he had given an informal talk, as if he were speaking to old friends around the fireplace.

Now radio stations around the country carried *President* Roosevelt's "chats." This let Roosevelt, relaxed and comfortable, friendly and plainspoken, come into homes everywhere and explain what he was trying to do. Each broadcast began with the words "My friends . . ." Franklin's plans were so complicated, they took a lot of explaining—and it took a lot of voter pressure on Congress to get the laws he wanted passed.

"All of my plans are designed to provide relief, recovery, and reform for America,"

he said. First he asked for help for farmers. The AAA, or Agricultural Adjustment Administration, was formed to make sure farmers were paid fairly for their crops. The NRA, or National Recovery Administration, was designed to do the same for manufacturers. It set pay and work standards, limiting child labor and safety hazards at work.

Many of Roosevelt's programs took unemployed people and paid them to do valuable work. The Civilian Conservation Corps, the CCC, paid thousands of unemployed young men to build roads and buildings, cut trails and restore lands in our national parks. The National Youth Administration, NYA, hired high school and college students to work in libraries and as research assistants so they would not have to drop out of school to go to work full-time. The WPA, or Works Progress Administration, hired construction workers and architects to build bridges and roads. It hired artists and musicians, writers and sculptors, too, for thousands of different projects countrywide. It startled many people that the WPA insisted on paying blacks at exactly the same pay scale as white workers, but Roosevelt insisted on equal pay for equal work.

One of his biggest programs, the Tennessee Valley Authority, or TVA, funneled money into building dams throughout the South to create both construction jobs and affordable electricity for poverty-stricken rural folks like his friends in Warm Springs.

Franklin Delano Roosevelt's New Deal involved so many programs known by three letters that the press gave him the three-letter nickname, FDR. As money began trickling through the American economy again, people's love grew for their FDR. When a New York newspaper reported that he needed a swimming pool at the White House to help with his exercise program, children everywhere sent in nickels and dimes. The swimming pool was installed during the first year he was in office.

And still the ideas flowed from the White House. At Franklin's urging, Congress set up a Social Security system where a little bit of every employee's paycheck—and the employer's, too—is held in a special fund. When a worker is disabled or becomes too old to work, that money is paid back. Another program for workers was Roosevelt's National Labor Relations Board. It helped set standards for labor unions and industries.

FDR seemed to be everywhere. On weekends he went to Hyde Park or to a presidential retreat in Maryland, Shangri-La, now called Camp David. He cruised about on navy vessels and journeyed to Warm Springs, too. As much as he traveled, Eleanor traveled more. She brought him valuable information about what she had seen and what people were saying around the country. When they spoke of FDR now, some people were angry.

Poor people everywhere saw the benefit of his plans. They loved FDR. Rich people were not happy at all. They felt that his New Deal was a bad deal for them. They complained that all the projects around the country were not necessary. They thought his fair labor laws were meddling in their businesses. They resented the regulatory laws and boards like the SEC—the Securities and Exchange Commission. It was designed to police the stock market so that a Black Thursday would never happen again, but it put limits on what the rich could do to get richer.

But still the ideas flowed from the White House, or wherever FDR was. His cabin down at Warm Springs took on a new name: "The Little White House." While it had only six rooms, it did have white pillars out front like the president's mansion in Washington. Franklin spent hours in the marvelous waters of Warm Springs, exercising and learning new exercise therapies to practice in his own pool at the White House. When he could, he would sneak away from his Secret Service guards and drive alone to the top of Pine Mountain and drink in the view of trees and hills and rich red dirt. It never failed to restore him.

In 1934 he threw a party for the Georgia Warm Springs Foundation. "Come celebrate my birthday," he said to his rich, important friends. "We're going to try to raise a little money for research toward a cure for polio." Every year thousands of people were still being stricken with the dread disease, and science seemed no closer to finding a cure. Roosevelt had changed how polios were treated in therapy. He was showing, every day, how wrong it was to hide the disabled away in shame. Now he was determined to do all he could to find the cure.

Other people heard about the fund-raiser and decided to hold parties of their own. In the end there were "birthday balls" for FDR all over the capital and over a million dollars was raised for polio research by year's end. The next year, even in the slow, depressed economy, more balls were held and more money raised.

Things weren't going as well, politically. The Supreme Court struck down his program to help farmers, the AAA. They also ended his business-labor program, the NRA. Both of these, they said, went against the Constitution of the United States. There was nothing Franklin could do about it. There were nine judges. They did not like his programs and they would keep striking them down as long as they were in office—and they would be in office until they died.

Millions upon millions of Americans had been helped by Roosevelt's programs by the end of his first term in office. These were the common people—the farmers and workers, the children and wage earners. They would vote for him for another term. Still, the election was a fight—the kind Roosevelt loved. He had turned the tide of the Great Depression, but his enemies said he had become a dictator. They said the taxes he had placed on the rich were ruining them. The wealthy resented the help others were getting. It was un-American, they said. Their hatred grew as they imagined the money they could have been earning if FDR hadn't brought his New Deal to the American people.

Roosevelt won the 1936 election by a landslide. He had great plans for his second four years as president. The New Deal had gone well—what he had been able to get into law. But Congress was beginning to listen to the complainers instead of the common people. And the Supreme Court was listening to no one.

FDR wanted the Supreme Court to change so it would let him do what he wanted. The Constitution said that when the old judges retired, he could name new ones. He would choose ones friendly to his causes of course. But none of the old judges seemed interested in leaving yet, and FDR did not want to wait.

A president cannot just fire the justices, but Roosevelt had an idea. Couldn't he just add enough new ones to shift the votes to his favor? It was a daring idea. It wasn't quite right—but it just might work. FDR tried to get laws passed that would allow him to appoint a new judge for every judge over seventy years old. He reminded everyone that the number of justices on the Court had been changed before, seventy years earlier. He tried to make the change sound constitutional.

The risks he had taken before had worked out well for himself and for the country. This one was bad for both. Members of Congress were furious with this power grab. They voted it down and spent the rest of his term voting down his other ideas. Roosevelt's enemies pointed to his efforts to change the Court to prove that he was power crazed. The move cost him many of his loyal voters, too.

Still, there were lights in thousands of southern homes thanks to him. People were employed and farms were making money again. Banks were solid and Social Security protected people. The national parks had become places to be really proud of. Franklin was still beloved for what he had managed to do, but the only new programs he could get through Congress in his second term were a minimum wage for all workers, a workweek limited to forty hours, and the end of using children as workers in factories.

For his birthday in 1937 there were seven thousand balls given around the country! Three million Americans partied—and donated money to finding a cure for polio. Wealthy Democrats had run most of the balls. The numbers were exciting, but they were also worrisome. It had begun to look as if polio were a Democratic Party cause. The economic woes of the country made buying a ball gown or tuxedo too expensive for most people. Roosevelt's enemies were beginning to make fun of Warm Springs and the silly birthday balls that supported it.

Anyone anywhere could get polio, and Roosevelt felt that everyone everywhere should pitch in to help end it. By fall he announced the end of his birthday parties. He was founding a nonpolitical organization to fund treatment of polio victims and to support research by doctors like the young Jonas Salk. The National Foundation for Infantile Paralysis had a board of directors made of wealthy men from *both* political parties.

Eddie Cantor suggested that the fund-raiser be called the March of Dimes. A newspaper picked up the idea and asked children to send dimes to the White House. Almost anyone could "spare a dime" by now. Cantor sang about it on the radio. The Lone Ranger asked for donations, too, during his radio show.

At first the response was discouraging. Then one day the White House got thirty thousand envelopes in the mail, and in each envelope was a dime. The White House staff piled the sparkling silver dimes on tables and stared at them. Each of the coins, with Liberty's head on one side and a bundle of rods on the other, meant that somewhere a child cared about ending polio. There were little wings on Liberty's cap, so she looked like Mercury, the winged god of ancient Rome. People called these coins Mercury dimes and they began flying into the White House.

The next day fifty thousand dimes arrived. The next, one hundred and fifty thousand envelopes filled the mailroom, each with a small donation inside. The March of Dimes had become an avalanche.

The White House mail chief said, "The government of the United States darn near stopped functioning," as all available hands were put to opening letters. The president's children, secretaries, and assistants went to work on the piles of mail. WPA writers and artists were paid to come in and help. FDR laughed with glee. By the end of 1938, $1,800,000 had been raised, dime by dime. Franklin's second term was beginning to look like a success after all. Polio was killing and crippling millions of people around the globe and FDR had found a way to fight the disease. He had always loved a battle, and this was a war he intended to win!

"Doctor Win-the-War"

Franklin Roosevelt was not the only strong leader of a major world power in 1938. In Germany Adolph Hitler's power was growing by the day, and another dictator, Benito Mussolini, had taken control of Italy. Either of them would do anything to get more power. They both had led their countrymen into battles against other nations to get the land, the resources, and the power that they wanted. Germany had invaded Austria and Czechoslovakia, areas set aside after the "War to End All Wars" as demilitarized zones. Italy's armies had marched into Ethiopia in northern Africa and brutally taken over. Worse yet, these two hungry rulers had teamed up as the "Axis" powers, and they were threatening to invade Spain together.

Americans knew most of what was happening. FDR had told them in fireside chats. It was in the newspapers, too. But people felt other countries would just have to solve their own problems. Economic troubles had been an epidemic around the globe, and it had left people everywhere weakened and struggling to survive. This made it easy for evil leaders to persuade others to follow them with the promise of security and triumph.

Warlords in Japan had declared a "Greater East Asia Co-Prosperity Sphere." They had led their armies into battles throughout Korea and Manchuria. Having expanded their power base, they started a vicious invasion of China.

Now FDR's knowledge of Europe and his contacts around the world paid off. He met with leaders whenever he could and discussed plans to avoid war. Some he met on boats. Others came to the White House. The queen and king of England traveled to Hyde Park. They stayed at a little cabin he had built for himself away from the formal mansion there. Roosevelt introduced the queen to hot dogs. For a moment she searched around the table for a fork and knife. Surely she was not expected to *touch* her food? "What am I to do with this sausage?" she finally asked.

"Just open your mouth, push it in, and chew," he told her, and grinned. The queen followed directions, and loved it. FDR had an easy charm that made people relax around him. Winston Churchill, now England's prime minister, had become friends with Franklin as soon as the men met.

Ever present beneath the enjoyable social whirl of Franklin's life was his polio. Nothing he did was easy. His busy schedule had to allow time for daily therapy sessions. Except for his exercise time, every moment of every day was spent strapped tightly into heavy, hard steel from his waist down. He sat, leg braces locked in one chair, for as long as he could manage before the time-consuming task of moving. Then he shifted into a wheelchair he had designed. It was little more than a kitchen chair with wheels on its legs. It had no arms to hold him in and no brakes, but it was slender enough to fit through doors easily and fit under his desk.

FDR looked at the reports coming across that desk with growing horror. So many people were in danger around the world! Hitler's German troops were targeting Jews and Gypsies and homosexuals—Germany's own citizens. There were reports of beatings and killings. Yet Americans were reluctant to lend anybody a hand. When Roosevelt pleaded to relax immigration levels so the frightened victims abroad could come here for safety, the answer was a swift no from Congress. Jobs were scarce and no one wanted a flood of foreigners competing for space in our fragile economy. Roosevelt organized an international conference to try to find safe homes for people that Hitler had targeted. Only Denmark and Holland were willing to take in the refugees.

On November 9, 1938, Hitler had his troops attack Jews throughout Germany and Austria. In a night of mob violence, they smashed shops and homes, destroyed synagogues and schools, and killed nearly a hundred people. By morning the streets were full of broken glass. More horrible still: Thirty *thousand* people were missing. It took time to find out where they'd gone, and, even then, many did not believe it. All those people had been taken to concentration camps, where they worked as slaves until they died or were simply killed. Hitler had said these people were not pure enough to be part of his dream of a perfect Germany, a Germany that would take over the world.

Roosevelt told reporters that he could "scarcely believe that such things could occur in a twentieth-century civilization." He bent laws to allow thousands of Germans to flee to the United States, though many thousands more were left behind, trapped.

On September 1, 1939, German troops stormed into Poland, leaving a path of destruction. On the third, Britain and France declared war on Germany. "When peace has been broken anywhere," Franklin said in that night's fireside chat, "the peace of all countries everywhere is in danger." He meant the United States, but people still wanted to stay isolated from the danger of battles. On September 17 the Soviet Union attacked Poland from the east and the country soon fell.

Next Denmark fell after a bloody attack. Norway, too, fell to the German troops.

Franklin ached to help his allies stand up to the Germans, but he could not even sell them weapons because of the Neutrality Act that Congress had passed in 1937. Americans watched in disbelief as German soldiers fought their way into Holland and Belgium and overpowered those countries, too.

Roosevelt pushed hard at Congress and they finally repealed the Neutrality Act. The new law replacing it said that our allies could buy any weapons they wanted, so long as they paid for them in cash and took them away in their own ships. Now he could help! And now Germany moved to invade France.

FDR's second term as president was almost up. Now was the worst time to change leaders, he told everyone. Then he announced he would run again. Many Americans were horrified at the thought of a three-term president. "Does he want to be dictator?" they asked. But without much of any campaign, they reelected him by a huge margin. After seeing bloody battlegrounds from the First World War, FDR hated the very idea of war, but he knew he was the right leader to steer the nation through whatever was coming.

He expected war. He did not expect death. Mother Roosevelt died before she could see her son take the presidential oath on the old Bible again. The rock beneath his life was gone, suddenly. Hyde Park was empty, and so was that part of his soul.

"May I be left alone for a few moments?" he asked as he held a box of treasures found in her bedroom. His eyes filled as he looked over letters from him as a little boy, locks of his baby hair, school trinkets, and photos. Within a few hours he wheeled out of the room. Besides putting on a black armband, there was no time for more grief.

Winston Churchill sent a frantic message to FDR, begging for help. The Germans were bombing England. If somebody didn't help, they would be the next country to fall to Hitler.

England was out of everything—supplies and weapons and money, too. He couldn't pay for weapons to save his own country.

Roosevelt thought hard about what he could do to help his friend and to save England. Hitler had to be stopped! Finally he decided to "bend" the laws again because, as he explained, "even another day's delay may mean the end of civilization." Roosevelt sent fifty old but usable destroyers sailing toward England. He also got Congress to raise an army by starting the draft of young men to be soldiers and sailors. Money was approved for weapons, uniforms, and training. Though three-quarters of United States citizens still yearned to isolate themselves from the war, most of them knew now it was coming.

On January 20, 1941, FDR took the oath to be president for the third time. His speeches now were all about the war. German forces had slammed through Yugoslavia and Greece. Now they were marching toward Russia.

Churchill and Roosevelt sneaked away from

their countries to hold a secret conference on a warship off the coast of Newfoundland, Canada. They agreed to form an "Atlantic Charter," fighting together for the "Four Freedoms" FDR had outlined in his State of the Union speech earlier that year: freedom of speech, freedom of religion, freedom from want, and freedom from fear for all peoples of the world.

In March the Congress finally loosened the rules for sending weapons to help in the war. They could be loaned out, they said, or leased, to countries under aggression, and kept for as long as they were needed. This lend-lease law untied FDR's hands so he could send materials for fighting against the Axis powers. But he could not yet send soldiers into the war for freedom.

On December 7, 1941 war came to the United States. Japanese planes attacked Hawaii, dropping bombs and firing torpedoes on Pearl

Harbor. It was early Sunday morning. There was no warning. Almost the entire the Pacific Fleet of the United States Navy lay at anchor. Most of the sailors were sound asleep when the attack began. Many never woke up.

Twenty-four hundred Americans were killed in the attack. Three hundred forty-seven planes were bombed on the runways. The fleet was crippled, with nineteen warships sunk or damaged.

Roosevelt listened to the news with fury. Americans everywhere responded the same way. The United States was done with isolationism.

The next day, FDR gave a speech to the Congress. It is rare for both senators and representatives to come together, but there wasn't an empty seat in the House chamber as James, now a captain in the marines, walked his father in. Suddenly everyone was standing, showing by applause that they were united behind this man.

He stood in his braces, legs locked, face serious. He called December 7 "a date which will live in infamy." He told the Congress—and through the radio, the rest of the country—the details of what had been done to the American forces. Within minutes the Congress had declared war on Japan.

The same day, England also declared war on Japan in support of the United States.

Three days later Germany and Italy declared war on the United States.

In January FDR stood before Congress again to give his annual State of the Union address. Instead of looking as desperate as the country felt, he seemed almost cheerful. Once before, his optimism and wild ideas had gotten the country out of a depression. Now his positive attitude reassured everyone. When he calmly set impossible goals for the country—make 75,000 tanks in 1943 and 125 airplanes, too—people didn't complain. They straightened their backs and threw everything into meeting the quotas he had set, and more.

FDR stayed with the people, sharing his courage and calm through more fireside chats. He wanted to be called "commander in chief" now, not just "president"—and no one minded. He had tough decisions to make. One of the first was what to do about the many thousands of Japanese immigrants and their children living in America. Many were citizens. Were any of them spies for the Japanese government? Were they all? How would you tell?

Some people were calling for them all to be rounded up and put into camps. "They could be watched there," they told the president. FDR did not want to do anything that sounded like the concentration camps in Germany. "Of course," he was told, "these people would not be hurt. And they'd be let go as soon as the war was over." In the end he agreed to the forcing of Japanese Americans into detention camps.

The war effort changed many things in America. There were clear enemies and every American agreed that they must be fought. Patriotism colored everything now. Men volunteered to serve long before they were drafted. At its peak, fifteen million served in the armed forces. So many men were fighting in Europe and the Pacific that there weren't enough left at home to run the factories.

Up until the war, jobs had been so scarce that any woman who took one was thought to be "stealing" it from a man who needed it for his family. Women stayed home, told that they were fragile and in need of a man to support them. Now, for the first time, women were welcome to try "man's work" and get paid for digging ditches, working in mines, and bending metal sheets into shape, then riveting them into airplanes. One famous poster made "Rosie the Riveter" into a heroine—attractive, strong, and patriotic.

Segregation had been the rule, too. In many

places "Jim Crow" laws governed blacks, keeping them out of restaurants, movie theaters, schools, and jobs where whites were welcome. FDR had insisted that blacks be paid the same as whites. Now he made another wild announcement. Discrimination against blacks in government and defense industries would be against the law.

Whites who were used to feeling "above" everyone else found themselves fighting alongside blacks whose contributions on the battlefield were equally important. Like the women who had been told they were incapable, blacks had always been told they were inferior. Now that both groups had seen the door open to another way of living, they would strive never to go back to their old roles.

For all of the effort and all of the spirit, the war did not go well at first. American soldiers died by the thousands, fighting the Japanese on Pacific islands. In Europe their shattered bodies were buried in vast graveyards where they fell. They gasped their last breaths in northern Africa, too, in battles that the Axis powers won. Families who had lost someone in battle were allowed to post a gold star on their homes. Some houses had three or four, and still the war raged on.

Roosevelt did everything he could to keep the nation's spirits up. He traveled as much as possible, always with his flashy cape, his cigarette at its cheery angle, and now with Fala. His dog, a little black Scottish terrier, looked as spunky as the president himself. FDR and Fala traveled to a hospital in Hawaii. He especially wanted to visit the amputee ward. Soldiers whose battle wounds were so bad that arms or legs had to be cut off were sent there. These young men now were suddenly and forever handicapped.

Franklin didn't waste time just telling them to keep a positive attitude. He let them all see that he was handicapped, too. For once

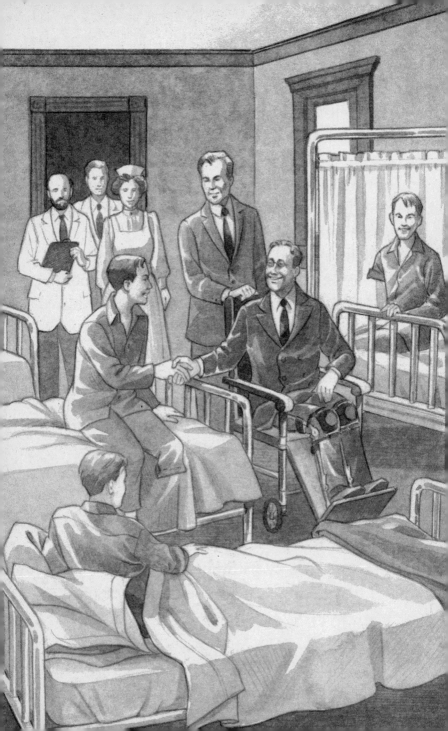

he let himself be wheeled up and down the aisles between the beds, his braces and withered legs in plain sight and a big grin on his face. Words alone would never have shown the men what Franklin had discovered for himself—a disability does not end a life.

Where he couldn't go, Eleanor went, poking and prying and asking the tough questions she knew he would want answered. Always his ears and eyes away from home, she was his right hand in wartime, inspecting defense plants and military bases, shipyards and factories. The sight of her brought people as much cheer as FDR himself. She always had a kind word for everyone and she *listened*. People knew she would take their messages to her husband.

Everyone leaned on Franklin. Newspapers called him "Doctor Win-the-War." Americans needed his energy, his determination, and his ideas. "All right," he would say to his secretary when yet another request came through, "send it over to me. My shoulders are broad. I can carry the load." But the strain was beginning to tell. Franklin could not get to a pool to swim as often as his body needed. He did not have time for as much daily therapy as the doctors prescribed. He stopped spending so much time upright in his braces. Now he sat as he commanded the war.

Everyone pitched in to help the war effort. People planted "victory gardens" so they could grow their own vegetables. That way the farm-grown crops could go to "our boys." All the rubber in the country was needed for tires on military jeeps and trucks, so everyone else had to do without. Silk was needed for parachutes, so women gave up silk stockings. There were food shortages, too. It wasn't long before a rationing system was put into place to make things fair. Everyone was given coupons each month. There were coupons for meat and for flour, for shoes and for gasoline. When

Americans bought any of these things, they had to hand in their coupons along with the cash. There were no more until the next month. Rationing was hard, and it took planning to do without, but it was all part of the war effort.

Stories flowed freely of the dreadful things our enemies were doing: prisoners starved and killed, horrible tortures, spy rings and scandals, whole villages destroyed. Rumors flew about the concentration camps in Germany. Millions of people were being shipped into the camps, but none were ever seen coming out. Where had they, or their bodies, gone? It was hard to believe that anyone would kill so many people. The State Department said it wasn't happening. And no one could get close enough to see.

When Franklin finally got the news that the concentration camps were really *death* camps, and worse than anyone had imagined, he created the War Refugee Board. By the end of the war, it had saved two hundred thousand Jews and twenty thousand others.

Finally he was able to share good news about the war during his fireside chats. Hitler's progress had been stopped and he was beginning to lose battles. The Japanese, too, had taken huge losses in the Pacific.

Some news, though, was never shared. Only Roosevelt and a few others knew about the secret weapon that was being developed under the code name the "Manhattan Project." It was a bomb more fearsome than anything humans had ever designed before, and Roosevelt hoped never to have to use it.

Other presidents had stayed in Washington during wartimes. Franklin traveled. He crossed the country by rail in 1942, traveling seven thousand miles. Along the way he held meetings, sometimes with local military and police, once with the president of Mexico. No matter how hard the Secret Service tried to hide his plans, Fala always gave them away. At every train stop, he had to get out and go on a walk. Someone was sure to see the little dog, and *everyone* knew who Fala was. The Secret Service just called him "The Informer."

FDR sailed away from his office, too. He crossed the Pacific to visit Hawaii and he crossed the Atlantic several times. It put him out in his beloved sea, but meant that he had to be carried up and down between ship and dock. When Franklin had to move from one ship to another, he was quietly loaded into a small boat up on the ship's deck. The little boat was lowered to the water. Lines were dropped from the ship he needed to board, the boat was attached and hauled upward to the deck. Through all of FDR's travels, he stayed in touch with war developments by telephone, telegraph, and telex.

He was hearing only good news now. The enemies were being beaten back. In 1943 he flew to North Africa to meet with Churchill. The war was going so well that they were deciding what terms of surrender they would accept from the Axis powers and Japan.

Later that year Franklin and Churchill met with Chiang Kai-shek, the Chinese leader. Japan had murdered millions of Chinese prisoners in a holocaust much like the one that Jews and others were suffering at Hitler's hands. From there they flew to Iran to meet with the Russian leader, Joseph Stalin. All the pieces were in place, he thought. "As long as these four nations with great military power stick together in determination to keep the peace," he told the country in a fireside chat, "there will be no possibility of an aggressor nation arising to start another war."

June 6, 1944, or "D day," Allied forces stormed the beaches at Normandy, France. The American general Dwight D. Eisenhower led the harrowing assault and the march to free Paris that followed. All around the world, the Allies were winning. The end was in sight!

Commander in Chief

Right when every war plan was coming together, Roosevelt felt like he was falling apart. He was tired, bone tired. He had not swum or exercised regularly in so long that his muscles were weakening, even those untouched by polio. He didn't complain. It wouldn't do to make a fuss right at the end like this. He just wanted to see this Second World War through to its end—world peace.

His third term was coming to an end more quickly than the war. "You *can't* quit now," his friends said. They had been with him for twelve years in the White House. Many, like Missy, his doctor, and Eleanor had been with him longer. They pleaded with him to try for a fourth term. A run for the governorship had pulled him out of his depression over polio once. They thought that another campaign was just what he needed to set him right now. Besides, they all liked being attached to this great man in the White House.

There were some howls of outrage outside the White House when he announced his decision to run again. "He's had the office long enough!" "He isn't well—never has been." "Who does he think he is?" But other voices cried with joy. FDR had gotten them through the Great Depression and kept them safe in a war. He had done everything he could for the common man, and they hadn't forgotten it.

Harry S. Truman agreed to run as his vice president and together they campaigned. Franklin let Truman make all the speeches and do the traveling. There was still a war to fight. The voters would understand, he said, if he put his attention there instead.

The voters did understand and, in November of 1944, voted him into a record-breaking fourth term. He paraded through cheering crowds with Fala in his open car in Manhattan and again in Washington, D.C. Both parades were held in pouring rain.

When it came time to choose the men and women who would be working with him for this term, he hesitated. He was upset that Churchill had met with Russia's leader, Stalin, and worked out a treaty while Roosevelt was campaigning for his reelection. Franklin knew exactly how he wanted the treaties written, and he wanted to be there.

But first he went to Warm Springs for a rest. The southern heat and the mineral waters made him feel a bit better, but food didn't taste good to him. His blood pressure was uneven and he was losing weight. But he had good news to announce. The March of Dimes had, by now, raised nearly nineteen million dollars. So many people had participated in the fund-raising, dime by dime, that the whole country seemed to be working toward the goal of finding a cure for polio. Millions of the dollars had gone into research. Millions more had gone into making other modern treatment centers for polio victims like the one at Warm Springs.

Back at the White House for a Christmas-time fireside chat he was able to sound cheery and hopeful for all the Americans who were listening to him over the radio. In January he was sworn into office. He insisted that all six of his grandchildren attend and watch him place his hand on the old Bible. His inaugural address was very short. Among other things he said, "Today, in this year of war, 1945, we have learned lessons—at a fearful cost—and we shall profit by them. We have learned that we cannot live alone at peace . . . our own well-being is dependant on the well-being of other nations."

Two days later FDR quietly left the White House and slipped into the cruiser *Quincy* for the trip to Yalta and his meeting with Churchill and Stalin. Like any old sailor, he found the trip across the stormy Atlantic Ocean relaxing. The flight to Yalta and the drive to meet the Russian leader was exhausting. Roosevelt had a head cold and had to leave his mouth partly open to breathe. That, and his poor color, made him look very ill.

Sick or not, Roosevelt argued for a strong United Nations where all the countries of the Earth could meet to talk out their problems instead of ever having to go to war again. Everyone agreed with him and plans were made to begin work on the peacekeeping body in San Francisco in the spring.

The other item of business to be settled

was how to manage Europe once the Germans were finally defeated. Stalin seemed determined to get as much land as he could for Russia. They argued back and forth and finally reached a compromise.

Stalin pledged to help now in the war against Japan. Since the Japanese soldiers seemed to be suicidal, no one knew how the fighting would ever end. The Allies needed every bit of help they could get if they were going to convince the Japanese to give up.

"We have wound up the conference—successfully I think," Franklin wrote to Eleanor days later. "I am a bit exhausted, but really all right."

On the way home the cruiser stopped in many ports. At each one FDR held meetings and entertained local leaders. At each stop he looked worse.

"You would be better off," his doctor said to him when he got home, "if you saved your strength and didn't see so many people." It was just the wrong prescription. Roosevelt needed the exercise of swimming, and physical therapy, and he needed the excitement of people around all the time. All three joys had been taken from him and his health was suffering more.

Warm Springs called to him. He traveled there in March for the comfort it always gave him. "I can be trim again," he assured a worried Harry Truman, "if I stay there for two or three weeks."

Once again the warmth and comfort of the Little White House at Warm Springs worked wonders on Roosevelt. He labored over his stamp collection, visited with his Georgia friends, and drove to the top of Pine Mountain to soak in the beauty of the scene he so loved. Back at the cabin on April 12, 1945, he sat chatting quietly with a circle of dear old friends. While he worked on papers at a table, an artist was making a portrait of him. She had just painted the proud tilt of his head and the dark shadows under his eyes when he suddenly rubbed his forehead. "I have such a headache," Franklin said, and collapsed.

He was carried to his bed, where he died quietly a few hours later.

Everywhere around the world, Franklin's friends mourned the passing of the great man. His funeral was planned so that as many people as possible could pay their respects. His body was placed on the Roosevelt train and sent northward, but slowly. For hundreds and hundreds of miles, people lined the tracks, standing silently or quietly crying. Eleanor, who had gone to Warm Springs to accompany Franklin home for the final time, could be seen through the windows sometimes. So could the Roosevelt children or plucky little Fala. But it was the president that the crowds yearned to see again, grinning and clamping that jaunty cigarette holder in his teeth. The

train stopped in Washington for a memorial ceremony, then steamed on to Hyde Park. As he had wished, Franklin Delano Roosevelt was buried on the hill overlooking the Hudson River, in the middle of his mother's rose garden.

After Roosevelt's death Harry Truman became president. Within a few weeks Hitler knew his twisted dreams of glory were over, and he killed himself. The dreadful weapon—the atomic bomb—that Roosevelt had kept secret was finally used when nothing else would convince the Japanese to stop fighting. Dropped on Hiroshima and Nagasaki in early August, the awesome power of these bombings forced Japan to surrender and ended the Second World War.

Nine months after Roosevelt's death, the United Nations opened its first session in England. Eleanor Roosevelt was there as a delegate from the United States. She became the chair of the U.N. Commission on Human Rights. Every committee and peacekeeping force of the United Nations is a kind of memorial to the man who loved a good political fight, but hated war.

There are many memorials to Franklin Delano Roosevelt that you can visit. One is in Washington, D.C. There are others at his homes in Hyde Park, New York; on Campobello Island, New Brunswick, Canada; and in Warm Springs, Georgia.

But the nearest memorial is right in your pocket. Within months after his death the United States changed the way dimes look. To this day FDR, the man who started the March of Dimes, appears on every newly minted dime.

When Franklin was stricken with polio, no one knew that it was spread through the air by a virus. They could only guess that swimming pools or water or chills or flies carried it from person to person. They didn't know what viruses were, or how they live and grow inside of cells, then make them burst. That is what destroys the nerve cells in the brain and spinal cord of polio victims.

In 1954 Dr. Jonas Salk, a researcher funded by Roosevelt's March of Dimes, created the first vaccine against polio. Given in childhood, it protected a person for life against catching polio—but it had to be injected deep into a muscle. A few years later, Dr. Sabine invented a polio vaccine that could be swallowed. Soon, every child in America had swallowed the oral vaccine. Its job done, the March of Dimes decided to fight different childhood diseases.

But the polio virus still infected children in other countries around the world. Only an international organization could fight it everywhere. Roosevelt's United Nations put two committees to work on the job, WHO, the World Health Organization, and UNICEF, the United Nations International Children's

Fund. Together they made up millions of doses of polio vaccine and brought them to children everywhere. The United States Centers for Disease Control and International Rotary Clubs joined the fight, too.

By the time you read this, the long battle against infantile paralysis may be over. FDR's greatest memorial may be the worldwide freedom from polio.

For More Information

Franklin Delano Roosevelt, by Russel Freedman, Clarion Books, 1990. This book contains many wonderful photographs of Franklin's life and times.

Eleanor Roosevelt, Fighter for Social Justice, by Ann Weil, Childhood of Famous Americans Series, Simon & Schuster, 1989.

America in the Time of F. D. Roosevelt, by Sally Senzell Isaacs, Heinemann Library, 2001. This book tells many more details of every day life in the depression and during World War II.

Jonas Salk and the Polio Vaccine, by John Bankston, Mitchell Lane Publishers, Inc., 2001. Learn how scientists, with FDR's backing, unraveled the mysteries of this dreadful disease.

198

On the Internet:

The Home of Franklin D. Roosevelt National Historical Site home page
http://www.nps.gov/hofr/hofrhome.html

The Roosevelt Campobello International Park Commission pages from New Brunswick, Canada. Beautiful photographs
http://www.fdr.net

Franklin Delano Roosevelt Presidential Library and Museum
http://www.fdrlibrary.marist.edu/index.html

The National Park Service site on The Franklin Delano Roosevelt Memorial in Washington, D.C.
http://www.nps.gov/fdrm/home.htm

For adult readers:

FDR's Splendid Deception, by Hugh Gregory Gallagher, Vandamere Press, 1999. The author of this book is a polio, so he brings a real understanding to the burden FDR carried.

Franklin D. Roosevelt: Rendezvous with Destiny, by Frank Freidel, Little Brown and Company, 1990. A detailed look at the politics and personalities of FDR's life.

No Ordinary Time: Franklin and Eleanor Roosevelt: The Home Front in World War II, by Doris Kearns Goodwin, Simon & Schuster, 1994. The beautifully researched and written Pulitzer Prize–winning look at their marriage and the world at war.